MONSTROUS TA

More long read

Edited by Dorothy Davies

MONSTROUS TALES – VOLUME 4
More long reads for late nights

GRAVESTONE PRESS

TABLE OF CONTENTS

Drink My Soul ... Please (Rie Sheridan Rose)

—what dreams may come must give us pause....
Hamlet, William Shakespeare

The machine sat on the scarred oak counter...a tiny monitor with battered keyboard. It looked so innocent, its cursor blinking steadily, a little green pulse tallying electronic heartbeats. A single word of text glowed on the screen invitingly. "Engage...?"

Daniscar Zenov jerked upright with a gasp, staring around him in the darkness.

Just another dream.... He buried his face in his hands. Dear God...no more dreams. Please...no more dreams.

***

Elianora Vaire could only just remember a time before the War. She had been ten when it started. When it began, they predicted it would be over in days—ending with the long-feared destruction of the world. Instead, it took eighteen years.

The problem of radiation poisoning had been licked with the invention of the Doomsday Bombs. Cities might fall, but the air would be safe for the Powers-That-Be when they crawled out from under their rocks, so they didn't hesitate to use the weapons. Civilizations that had stood for millennia were rubble in weeks.

Of course, there were things that those in power had failed to take into account. Such as the fact that military bases weren't the only things housed in cities. So were factories and refineries, universities and banks....

By the end of the second year, the armies were fighting on horseback and on foot. By the end of the third year, the major fighting was down to desultory strikes by bands of roving commandos. The ordinary citizenry who managed by luck or curse to survive the initial destruction of their world began to pick up the broken threads of tattered lives.

Elianora and her father, Tikardo, were near nobility in the tenuous power structure of the New World economy. Tikardo had two horses to draw the sawed-off truck bed that served as his traveling showroom. He was a metal dealer who sold most of his wares to farmers struggling to revitalize the countryside. A used car salesman in the Before War world, the gleanings from his devastated lot had seen them through the worst times with relative ease when his neighbors started trying to rebuild. Scrap metal was a precious commodity in a world thrown back to its roots.

Elianora stepped out of the three-room cinder block home that seemed palatial compared to others in the neighborhood. She swept dark hair from her forehead with the back of a well-tanned arm. Her hands were covered with flour. It was a day of celebration. Word of the Cease-Fire had come through with the morning's news-crier and she had decided to bake a cake. Not a true light and frothy confection like she vaguely remembered from childhood, but a treat for her father, nonetheless.

8

He was late. She expected him long before this. The day had been scorching hot. There might be no radiation, but dust clouds rising into the atmosphere from myriad bombings had never fully settled, making semi-tropics of formerly temperate areas. The cinder block dwellings stayed fairly cool, but having a cook fire inside would turn one into a kiln.

She set the pan containing her cake batter in the center of the outdoor convection oven and blew on red-hot coals. With a satisfied smile, she dusted her hands on her white linen shift and stood up, scanning the horizon once more.

On the edge of sight, she glimpsed a horse-drawn cart... but it was single harness, not her father's double rig. A salesman's signature toga fluttered in the light breeze beginning to stir as he waved to the girl by the cook fire. Her tall figure was well known to the whole village.

Elianora waved back and turned to step into the house. A piercing whistle stopped her in her tracks, and she spun to see Tikardo's cart approaching from the south. She ran to meet him. Her mother had died when she was five—long before the War started—and Tikardo was the only constant she remembered.

"Papa, is it true?"

He didn't need to ask for elaboration. "Yes, Angel, it's true. The War is over." He leapt lightly from the cart and enfolded her in a bear hug. "The War is finally over."

Tikardo was a big man, darkly handsome. When the War had begun, he was the same age that Elianora was now, and it had taken numerous favors and all of his pre-War savings to be mustered out as a

9

single parent. Many friends and relatives were not so lucky—a pain that gnawed at him daily—but one look at Elianora's shining face proved the cost worthwhile.

Thankfully, she remembered nothing of those first terror-filled War years... and he had paid dearly again to make it so.

"I have a surprise for you, Lia."

"What is it, Papa?" She glanced eagerly toward the rear of the cart.

"You'll get it tomorrow," he laughed.

"What is it?" she repeated, an edge of impatience rising in her voice—she was unused to delayed gratification.

"Dani's coming home."

***

In a temporary camp halfway across the village, War-weary soldiers enjoyed the first safe sleep many of them could remember. There was nothing left worth fighting for by the end of the fifth year... but duty dies hard, and no one ever said "stop." So the raids had gone on... and on... and on. Until the Powers-That-Be finally remembered the word "cease-fire."

There was a wistful quality to the air as the sun managed to break through the dust clouds just in time to set. The low arcing beams gave the utilitarian buildings fleeting warmth they aesthetically lacked.

Daniscar Zenov closed his eyes and breathed in the spring sunset.

Maybe tonight I'll sleep.

Lately he'd been too tired to sleep... and too afraid. With sleep came dreams and dreams were definitely something to be feared.

Dani could remember the time before the War much more clearly than former neighbor Elianora. He had been seventeen when the War began and keen to fight. It had seemed like the ultimate adventure to a headstrong teenager.

For more than half his life he had been a soldier. The adventure had worn off with his first scavenging mission into a newly bombed city. The death and destruction had left him violently ill—to the raucous amusement of his older comrades—and he had vowed then and there to survive the War at any cost.

It hasn't always been easy either, he reflected, absently massaging the right arm he had nearly lost three years ago.

But the scars he bore on his body could never touch those on his soul... Dani sighed, with a wry half-smile. Such thoughts did no one good. His left hand strayed to the chain around his neck and the battered locket that hung from it.

The talisman had kept him going through more than one rough spot. Without opening it, he could see the images inside. In one half of the locket rested a family portrait of a happy couple and a grinning blond teenager—how very long ago that photo session seemed—images from another life.

In the other was a picture hastily cut and wedged into the opening. It showed a dark-haired solemn-eyed little girl, trying so hard to look older than her ten years... He ran his good hand through lank blond hair that lay like bleached straw across his leathery forehead. A jagged scar ran from left cheek to temple. His gray-green eyes no longer laughed.

Will she even know me...?

He stepped to the doorway of the cinder block hut he was assigned to with the rest of his squad. With a sigh, Dani pushed aside the tinkling curtain of scrap metal serving as door, stooping to go inside.

Tomorrow I will find out...

***

Elianora pulled back in her father's arms. "W-what?"

"Dani's coming home. I saw him this afternoon. We're the closest thing to family he has left, so I invited him to lunch. He'll be here tomorrow about noon."

She walked to the cook pit in a daze, automatically checking the progress of her cake.   "Lia...?"

"Dani's coming home..." she whispered, one hand straying to neatly braided hair. "Excuse me, Papa."

She pulled the cake out of the oven, setting it on the edge of the pit to cool and continuing into the house.

She drifted into the small alcove Tiko had partitioned off for her. She went to the far corner and knelt before a rickety shelf upon which sat a small carved wooden box—one of the few mementos of her mother she still possessed.

She carefully unlocked the casket with a tiny key she wore around her neck. Inside the box was what

12

she possessed of Daniscar. She made herself comfortable on the floor and spread out her treasures one by one. There was a larger copy of the family photo in his locket, heavily creased from years when she had slept with it clutched tightly in her hand. A second photo showed a younger Dani tossing six-year-old Lia into the air as she squealed with laughter. A crumpled piece of paper wadded up in anger many years ago, then lovingly smoothed out declared LIA LOVES DANI FOREVER in careful block print. And there was the letter.

Tikardo had read it to her gently the first time because she wasn't able to decipher the scrawled cursive yet... and he held her close as she cried herself to sleep, only able to grasp that her beloved Dani was leaving her, and not the reason why. Not that she fully understood even now why the seventeen-year-old had lied his way into the army.

Later that night, she had quietly walked out of the house and run barefoot in her nightgown to tap urgently on his window.

Tearfully, she had forced her photograph on him, promising to wait forever... and now he was coming home. At last. She had never forgotten—or betrayed—her promise, but long ago despaired of keeping it when no word came.

Her vague memories were now older than Dani was when he left.

Does he even remember me after all the horrors he must have suffered?

Tomorrow she would find out...

***

13

Sleepless eyes of gray and brown greeted the hazy red dawn.

On opposite ends of the cinder block city, grateful sighs were heaved that daylight had finally come. For her part, Elianora pulled on a tunic that fell to mid-thigh, carefully dyed deep sky-blue with precious reserves scavenged from the old city. She fussed restlessly with her waist-length hair until Tikardo threatened to cut it off, then quickly plaited it into its customary braid.

Having no option but his uniform, Dani was already dressed, but even more apprehensive about his appearance. He took stock of it dubiously in a piece of polished tin. His uniform hung on him after six months of shortened rations. His face was hollow and gaunt—the grinning teenager all but wiped away from the grim soldier. His right arm dangled awkwardly, good for little more than steadying his rifle. He needed a haircut, but couldn't bear to waste time.

I have to know. And I have to know now.

He took up his rifle from habit too ingrained to lose easily, he started across town, following the directions Tikardo Vaire had given him. The merchant had offered to fetch him, but Dani had declined, wanting to get a feel for his new surroundings.

So much had changed since he was a boy that he wasn't ready yet to call it "home." And there was no denying he felt uncomfortable in the older man's presence—as if he had left something undone it might be too late to repair. It was a dreadful shock

14

to glance up from the campfire at noon yesterday and see Vaire staring at him as if he were a ghost. He recognized Vaire at once. There was much less change in a man between age twenty-eight and forty-six than there was between seventeen and thirty-five.

Seeing Vaire had brought so many memories flooding back—memories not tinged with the blood of the horrific War...

He had gone next door to Vaire's the night before he left to join the army and nervously approached Tiko. Lia was only ten—a baby—but he'd loved her all her life.

More afraid of being turned down than he was to fight, Dani had asked for Elianora's hand if he returned. Since no one expected the War to last more than a week or two, it was rather silly of him to ask.

Vaire kindly told the blushing teen as much—but gravely promised not to stand between them when she was old enough to decide for herself.

Dani wrote the letter then, sitting at Tiko's kitchen table, unable to face telling her in person he was leaving...

...And then the child had come to him on her own, tearful, but older than her years. She pressed the solemn-eyed portrait on him as a good luck token and vowed to wait forever if she must...

But eighteen years *was* almost forever. He'd tried to contact her at first... but the messages never seemed to get through.

In time, he gave up; sure she was dead... or married. It was too much to hope that her feelings remained unchanged.

Vaire did not mention a lover, but she is twenty-eight years old—surely she's had many suitors if she fulfilled the potential for beauty she showed as a child.

Dani shook his head to bring his thoughts back to the present.

In minutes he would know. He found the correct street among dozens the same by absently counting those he passed.

The cinder block structures were more elaborate here than those near camp, denoting wealth and status in the new economy. He slowed as he continued up the street, reluctant to finish the journey now he was so close.

There's the house.

Heart rose into throat at the sight of a lithe figure bending over the cook pit.

She is so beautiful... more beautiful than I ever could have imagined.

He almost turned and walked away—but she caught sight of him and raised a hand in tentative greeting. The gesture froze him in his tracks.

***

Lia glanced up from the cook pit to see a blond man in a ragged uniform standing a few yards away, rifle held loosely in one hand as he stared hungrily in her direction. Her first thought was he merely wanted food, and then she looked more closely. There was

16

an echo of the boy in the man—faint, but distinctive.

Her heart skipped a beat, and she raised a hand in greeting.

He is home. After what seems an eternity, Dani is really home!

The paralysis holding her broke and she ran to him, flinging herself into arms that automatically encircled her, then tightened painfully. She didn't mind.

"Dani, you came back!"

"Didn't I promise?" His voice was hoarse as he dropped his chin into her hair. "How could I have stayed away?"

"I was so afraid... but I waited. I always waited."

"I would have understood if you hadn't," murmured Dani softly.

She drew back enough to look up at him, bewildered by the remark. "How could I not? I promised too."

"I'll release you from your promise if you want me to."

She stared into his eyes, her confusion deepening. "But—"

"I don't have anything to offer you, Lia. A crippled soldier who doesn't even dare to sleep at night for fear he'll die in his dreams...."

"Please." She put fingertips to his lips. "Don't talk about it. Not now. Come, let's eat." She took his right hand, chin tilting defiantly as she did so and drew him to sit beside the cook pit. She casually adjusted her table arrangement to put things in easy reach of his left hand. She smiled at him as she went

17

to the fire. After a cursory check of the stew bubbling in its kettle, she slipped onto the bench beside him, ducking her head shyly.

"Lunch is almost ready."

"Thank you."

"You haven't tasted it yet," she replied ruefully, with a wry little grimace.

"No, I mean... thank you for being here to come home to." He raised his hand to her cheek, drinking in her face eagerly. "The hope you would be waiting eased me through more nights than you'll ever know."

She covered his hand with hers. "It's like a dream—"

"Please." He closed his eyes with a shudder. "Don't say that."

"Dani, what's wrong?"

He smiled wanly, in a vain attempt to reassure her. "Nothing, I'm fine."

"I think the stew should be ready." She rose in one smooth motion and moved back to the cook pit.

Lia stirred the stew, then ladled some into a large bowl and set it in front of him. "I don't claim to be a good cook," she warned, serving herself a smaller portion.

He blew on a spoonful of the stew and tasted it. "It could use a little salt," he admitted.

"Oh!" She raised hand to mouth, eyes wide. "I forgot."

He laughed—a lilting chuckle gone rusty with disuse. The sound grew into a full-throated roar, tears rolling down his cheeks as he tried vainly to control himself.

Lia looked on in puzzled bemusement, one finely shaped eyebrow cocked. "Dani—?"

"Oh, Lia," he finally managed to choke out, "how I've missed you." He held out his hand, and she moved eagerly into the circle of his arm.

"I've missed you too, Dani," she sighed, resting her head on his shoulder.

***

His laughter suddenly died in his throat. He gulped, tilting her face towards him and gazing down at the trust in her eyes. Suddenly, as if reaching a decision, he bent and kissed her parted lips.

Lia gave a muffled little cry. Dani jerked back.

"No—" she protested, "don't stop!" She threw her arms around his neck and pulled his mouth back down to hers. "I've wanted to do this for so long," she murmured against his lips, returning his kiss hungrily.

Dani lost himself in the kisses. His hands strayed to her hair, face and breasts, as if to convince himself she was real.

With extreme difficulty, he reined himself in before he allowed it to go too far.

I have to remember she is only a—but then, she isn't a little girl anymore, is she? She is a grown woman, with needs and desires of her own.

What are those needs? And will I be able to fill them?

He pulled away from her, looking down at her closed eyes and parted lips. A delicate flush of rose glowed beneath tanned cheeks.

She was eminently desirable.

God, how I want her...in more ways than one.

But in his mind's eye, he kept seeing that solemn-eyed little girl, and not this beautiful woman.

"Dani, what is it?" Her voice held tentative hurt. "Don't... don't you want me?"

"Oh, my precious girl—more than you could ever know!"

"Am I doing something wrong? I—I haven't had any practice." She swallowed hard, the flush in her cheeks blooming scarlet, "but I can learn—"

"Oh, Lia!" He hugged her to him fiercely, wanting to protect her, never to let her go. "Sweetheart, we have plenty of time for me to teach you what you want to know. Now, I'm just glad to be home." He sighed deeply, searching for the words to help her understand. "It isn't you. It's me. I—I'm just not ready yet."

"Make it soon."

The words were whispered so softly that he almost missed them. "I will. I promise. But there's something I want you to have first." He reached to the bottom of the thigh pocket of his worn fatigues and pulled out a small paper- wrapped object.

"What is it?" she asked, taking the packet with trembling hand.

"Open it."

She carefully unfolded the paper to reveal a simple gold band with a tiny diamond inset. "Oh, Dani—I can't take this. It's too precious!"

"There is nothing more precious to me than you, Lia. It was my mother's. I know she'd want you to have it."

"Dani...."

He slipped the ring onto her left hand. "I know things are less formal these days, Lia—but I've been waiting to ask you this for such a long time now..." He got down on one knee with a self-deprecating laugh. "Lia, will you marry me?"

"I told you before, silly. Don't you remember?"

"I wasn't sure you would," he replied seriously.

A fleeting glimmer of something half-recalled flickered behind her eyes, then was gone.

"Of course I remember. You proposed to me the night you left—and that's when I promised to wait. Of course I'll marry you. Why else would I have waited all these years? Now, get up off the ground and eat your stew before it gets cold."

She picked up the saltshaker and shook it vigorously over his bowl.

"I think that ought to do it," he commented ruefully, swinging a leg over the bench. "You don't do anything by halves, do you, girl?"

"No," she replied, her intensity charging the words far beyond the question, "I won't."

He noticed the change of tense, but forced himself to focus on the stew. Otherwise things might rapidly slip beyond his control.

***

The afternoon passed in a blur. They had so much to say to each other—little things that had been stored away like jewels to be taken out and exclaimed over. Lia told him everything she could remember

21

about how things had been at home. He told her the few things about the forefront that weren't horrible.

She sensed volumes lying unspoken behind the light anecdotes, but dared not press him. *If he wants to tell me in time, he will. Though he doesn't have to suffer the memories himself either.*

"Dani," she began hesitantly when the sun was sinking once more towards sunset. "What do you know about General Cardikof's Stand-Down Edict?"

He tensed, left hand gripping hers with bruising force. "More than I want to know," he replied brusquely, the words charged with emotion.

She couldn't quite decide if it was anger—or fear.

"I don't want to talk about that tonight, Lia." He tried hard to smile, but managed only a twisted grimace.

"But Dani—the Desensitizer—"

"No, Lia! Please...." He jerked his hand free and leapt to his feet. "I-it's getting late. I should go."

"But Papa will be home any minute—"

"Give him my regards, and my regrets." Dani snatched up his rifle and fled towards the road.

What did I say? The Desensitizer is a Godsend. It has done so much for so many people... and it seems to me like the soldiers will benefit most of all. She rubbed absently at the base of her neck. *It didn't do me any harm. What is Dani so afraid of...?*

***

Dani jogged through the darkening streets as if demons were at his heels. And, in a matter of

22

speaking, there were. Even the thought of the Desensitizer terrified him.

Created in the early stages of the War, the machine's weapon potential was soon declared inefficient. It didn't generate a wide enough field for mass application and subjecting individual enemy soldiers to the process was too time-consuming and impractical.

In the most basic terms, the Desensitizer erased memories, much like a computer program could be used to wipe a chip. The memories thus eradicated were irretrievably gone... and they would never even be missed.

That was the claim, at least. The doctors running the machine boasted the ability to remove as small a segment as a day, or a whole lifetime, as the situation demanded. It had become quite common for parents to exorcise the specters of War for their children through the miracle of the Desensitizer.

This was what Tiko had scrimped together credits for in those first tragic years of the War—he had paid to excise Lia's memories from her eleventh birthday until she was fourteen. Those were the days of worst destruction; without them, she remembered only the plodding day-to-day tedium of the raids. He had not tampered with the years before the War, but the gap helped dull the edges of her childhood...

Tiko confided this to Dani yesterday over a watery beer in a dimly lit tavern. It had sent a chill reverberating through him to hear the man speak so matter-of-factly about destroying a part of her soul. No matter how evil the memories, they belonged to *her*. To hear Lia casually suggest Dani do the same—it froze his blood.

God knows I can't sleep at night because the memories haunt my dreams...but they are a part of me. Can I live without them? Do I even want to try...?

Now General Cardikof, established as World Commander of the Unified Armies under the cease-fire, wanted all former soldiers to undergo treatment. His rationale was that removing the trauma of the War would make it easier for the men to rejoin society and lead productive lives.

Most of the War-weary combatants were jumping to sign up for the expensive treatment at government expense; his comrades in the barracks this morning could talk of nothing else.

But the thought that Dani kept coming back to—no matter how he tried to avoid it—was that with the memory of the War deleted from the world—and submission to the Desensitizer was ordered for *all* the Unified Armies—there would be no deterrent to starting it up again.

Now, the horror is so raw the very thought of another battle makes grown men shudder.

Such immediacy might wear off in time and the seeds of dissent blossom again in future, but the present—the here and now—is safe for the moment. The General's Edict might jeopardize that... intentionally or no. And deeper below that fear lay another. An insistent whisper in his very core asked, *What will he fill the void with if he takes away the War? What will happen to armies of men with eighteen years of their lives ripped away?*

24

Dani kept hearing a chorus running through his head—an old, old rock song that told of the headless specter of a mercenary stalking the night and firing his machine gun with the single-minded purpose of a zombie. Dani feared desperately that the General's plan would lead to the creation of an army of such soulless fighters.

The doctors won't be able to spend time picking and choosing among good days and bad for thousands of soldiers. They'll simply take away the entire block of time... and what will prevent them from wiping the rest of the slate clean while they are at it, giving the General those armies of zombie puppets for his amusement...

Dani found himself back at the barracks and ducked to enter.

He held back the tinkling curtain but stopped short in the doorway when he caught his name in the conversation going on just beyond the opening.

"Zenov could be trouble," growled a voice he couldn't place.

"Nah, Dani's a good guy," protested his friend Alexi.

"He's publicly questioned the General's order. It might make others question."

"He'll change his mind. Once he sees how much better it is for everyone, he'll come `round."

"What if he doesn't see?"

"Don't worry, I'll talk to him."

Dani eased the curtain carefully into position and backed away from the hut. Things were slipping away from him. Soon he might be forced to "come `round"—whether he liked it or not. He had to think.

He tightened his grip on the lifeline of his rifle and began wandering the dark streets of the ravaged city, searching for anything that might remain of his childhood. He passed the ruins of the school where his mother used to teach, abandoned playground marked by the jagged teeth of sawed-off metal poles, which once supported swings and monkey bars. Everything that could be scavenged for rebuilding had long ago been spirited away. He could almost hear the echoes of children playing and it caused him to hurry past with a shudder.

He passed a burnt-out husk that had once been the neighborhood library and gritted his teeth at the senselessness of it all.

There hadn't even been the excuse of political necessity for the War. The War need never have occurred at all.

The Consolidation had almost been complete before the first missile was launched. It had been a token protest from a handful of dissidents to begin with— and then bloodlust had taken root.

Dani indicated a secluded corner with twisted trees that had survived the War by virtue of decay, He huddled on the ground beneath their branches, resting his head on bent knees. Thoughts whirled through his tired brain as he tried to make sense of things.

He hadn't slept at all the night before, worrying about Lia's reaction to his rebirth and it had been days since he'd slept well... if not years. He hated sleep—fought it as long as he was able before slipping beneath its waters. Finally, however, despite all resolves, exhaustion won out and Dani slept...

The War had just entered its first winter. While the largest cities had been leveled months before, there were still smaller population centers like this one seeing their first bomb strikes. The squad was sent into the remains of a newly bombed apartment building to scavenge anything of potential value. Already food and ammunition were getting harder to count on as supply lines were constantly broken and reformed. Anything they found to supplement official rations was considered fair game.
``   Dani was gestured into a gaping doorway as the rest of the men fanned out. He had just passed his eighteenth birthday and already the glamour of war was beginning to pale. This was his first scavenging mission.
He ducked into the bombed-out apartment, gun clutched tightly in trembling hands, Dani moved slowly through ruined rooms. He picked up a small glass ornament and stowed it in the pocket of his fatigue jacket. It might fetch a few credits on the black market.
He started to relax a little. The dwelling appeared to be empty, and he breathed a sigh of relief. He was not really paying attention as he stepped through the kitchen doorway.
The crack of a pistol split the silence. Pain exploded in the side of his face and his finger tightened convulsively on the trigger of his rifle as he fell

backwards. He came to his senses to find his squad leader looming over him. "You alive, Zenov?"

"Y-yes, sir," he mumbled thickly, sitting up and reaching with fumbling fingers to explore the pain in the side of his head.

"It's just a crease, boy. Lots of blood, but no real damage. It'll scar, though—you'll have a nice memento there. Continue with your salvage, son. By the way—good shooting."

The sergeant clapped him on the shoulder and was gone. Dazed, Dani stumbled into the kitchen and dropped to his knees, swallowing hard against rising nausea. He lost the battle and was violently ill. Across the room, a small figure clutched a pistol in one lax hand. Half the child's face was gone as she slumped over a woman's stiffened corpse. The girl was no older than Lia... and he had killed her. She had been alone and afraid—no telling how long her companion had been dead—just trying to survive...

Dani moaned in his sleep. *How many nights must I see that blasted face in my dreams?*

It had gotten easier to accept the dead as the War dragged interminably on, but he never got over that little girl. To him, she symbolized the whole useless War. It was memories like this that haunted his dreams—that made the Desensitizer so alluring—but he couldn't give up the large part of his personality those memories shaped.

Without them he'd no longer be Daniscar Zenov, but someone, or some*thing*, else.

***

28

Lia's sleep was peaceful, her dreams of the future rather than the past. Lips curled in a smile, she dreamed of Dani and a little cottage of their own somewhere far away from the cinder block city…

In her dream, Dani was trying to plant a garden, "hepped" by a sturdy little boy about two with dark hair and gray-green eyes.

She sighed happily and turned over in her sleep—the dream shifted.

he saw herself cradling a baby in her arms as she corrected the pronunciation of the same little boy, now about five, while he read from a book clutched in chubby hands.

Dani came to stand behind her chair, laying his good hand on her shoulder and bending down to kiss her cheek....

There were no shadows in her dreams—Tiko had seen to that.

Her War memories were only of frustrated attempts to put together daily grocery needs and organize life around the deprivations. She didn't miss the images she no longer remembered. As far as she was concerned, she was the same Elianora Vaire she had always been and grateful to be so.

***

Dani woke when birds began to chirp in the predawn light.

He was stiff and cramped from sleeping sitting up all night and he rolled his head on his neck to ease the tension, wincing at the resulting pops. "I'm too old for this," he muttered, levering himself to his feet with his back against the tree. He straightened his uniform and shook his hair into place, running a hand through it as a final touch and his toilet was complete.

His rifle across his back, he started toward the main section of town. It was easier to think when he was moving, though he wasn't at all sure where to go. If he returned to the barracks, he would face Alexi's attempts to win him over—and if he continued to resist, the persuasion would not remain so friendly.

Every fiber of his being longed to head straight for Lia, but he hesitated. She did not understand why he was resisting the device any more than the army did.

His thoughts were whirling endlessly. He couldn't stop their roulette spin long enough to focus them on a solution. He had to center himself, before it was too late.

He spied an early morning cantina with smoke curling lazily from its cook fire. The heady scent of brewing coffee permeating the air made him decide to stop and rally his resources.

A worn 5-credit disk distracted him, so he flipped it on the table as he swung onto the bench. "Black, please."

The coffee was a fragrant cup of instant revival as he gratefully took a healthy swallow, then held the cup to his forehead. Somehow, despite the devastation, the world had managed to keep the coffee brewing—a testament to where priorities lay—and this was good coffee.

The thin, watery army brew was nothing like the deep, fresh taste of his youth and this was. The scent brought on another wave of memories. His mother in her sunny kitchen, turning to him with coffee pot in hand as they made ready to head for school in the morning. His father and Tiko arguing politics steam from their mugs rising between them while he and Lia played a complicated game of the child's invention. That first bitter sip of stolen caffeine, snatched from his father's cup when he was seven....

Memories.

He kept banging up against that wall. His memories were so much a part of him that he couldn't conceive of life without them.

Even the bad ones. He absently fingered the scar on his cheek. *What am I going to do...?*

He gulped the rest of his coffee and set down the cup with a deep sigh. The first thing he had to do was tell Lia goodbye.

It was the kindest thing to do. Knowing she was alive and well would have to be enough for him. *I need to disappear, and I can't ask her to go with me. It wouldn't be fair....*

***

"What do you mean 'it wouldn't be fair to you'?" Lia's eyes snapped fire. She tried to contain her anger, but it spilled over the top. "Daniscar Zenov, I've waited almost twenty years for you—wasted

31

two-thirds of my life dreaming of the day you'd come home and now—a few kisses, a little groping and you say 'okay, it's been fun, but I'm leaving now.' Well, you can rot in Hell for all I care, if that's the way you feel about it!" Her anger dissolved into bitter tears and she shook with the violence of her emotion.

Dani stood before her, shoulders bowed, reaching out, but not touching her, as if afraid of her reaction. He had surprised her when he knocked on the door—she hadn't been expecting him until later in the day and was flustered enough to see him. His news struck her to the core.

"I know I'm not very experienced, Dani—but I can learn. I don't know a lot about life, but I can keep a house neat and comfortable for you. I can cook... sort of. I—"

He held up a hand and shook his head. "Lia, it's not you. It's me. I can't stay. Don't you see?"

"No. Frankly, I *don't* see! Tell me. Explain it to me. I want to understand…"

He sank down onto the bench beside the fire. "I can't stay because I can't give in to them. I can't submit to the machine. I-I have to keep my memories—they are all that I have."

"You have me," she murmured softly, looking down at her hands so she wouldn't cry any more. "Aren't I enough?"

"Oh, baby, I wish I could say yes...but it would be lying to you and to myself."

"Did you or did you not give this to me yesterday afternoon and ask me to marry you?" She thrust out her hand and the tiny diamond flared like a beacon

32

in a shaft of sunlight. The light danced as her hand trembled. "Didn't you mean it?"

"Oh, yes... more than anything...." He caught her hand in his, "but I hadn't thought it through."

"Either you want to marry me or not. Whatever your decision, I will try and accept it, Dani... but let me say just one thing. I didn't wait eighteen years for you because I wanted a few kisses and a pat on the head. I waited for you because you meant more than anything else in the world to me... except maybe Papa. I waited for you because you told me you'd be back for me, and you never, ever lied to me, even when the truth hurt—like the time my kitten was run over and Papa said it ran away. You told me the truth and held me while I cried.

"You see! I haven't forgotten everything, just because of some silly machine. But if you think you need to run rather than accept the treatment, fine. Let's run. But, *please*, Dani—I beg you—let's do it together!"

"Oh, Lia, I do love you so." He held out his arms and she fell into them. "If you want to come with me, you can come. The thought of leaving you again was killing me."

"I can be ready in five minutes."

"No. I need to go by the barracks first and pick up my things... talk to some people. You need to speak to your father. He isn't going to like this..."

"I think you'll find him more sympathetic than you think, Dani." She grinned impishly. "Besides, this way he won't have to pay for the wedding."

"Meet me at the old school at sunset." He rose to go, lifting her to her feet as he stood. "We'll have to

33

travel light and go quickly... and we probably won't ever be coming back."

"As long as we go together, Dani. That's all I ask."

He kissed her hard. "The old school—at twilight. I love you, Elianora Vaire."

"And I love you, Daniscar Zenov—now go, before I decide not to let you."

He laughed and snatched up his rifle. "Twilight!" he called out as he backpedaled down the street.

"Turn around before you kill yourself!" she yelled back, one hand lifted in farewell.

When he was out-of-sight, she lowered her hand and clasped both of them in front of her. "Please let this work out," she prayed quietly. "He's been through so much."

"Miss Vaire?"

She turned at the sound of an unfamiliar voice behind her. "Yes?"

"I need you to come with me. I'm afraid there's been an accident."

"Dani—?" Her eyes flew to the direction in which he'd disappeared. Surely he hadn't been gone long enough to—

"No, Miss. It's your father."

"Papa! What happened?"

"There was an accident with his cart. I think you'd better come."

"Yes, of course." Without a second thought, Lia let herself be led away.

***

34

Dani made it to the barracks without seeing a single man in uniform. That in itself might not be so unusual... they had but newly returned to the city, maybe everyone felt the same need to re-familiarize themselves with their surroundings that had struck him the night before...

But the barracks themselves loomed empty as well. Not a single soldier stood sentry duty. No one lounged in front of the hut enjoying the sunlight. No one called out a greeting as he ducked inside the building.

Where is everyone? Did they all succumb to the lure of the Desensitizer? Even Alexi?

The thought shot a spur of pain through him. He and Alexi had been the youngest in the squadron—the other but a year ahead of him. They had banded together from the first against the tyranny of the older men. He had shared everything with Alexi, from his dreams to his rations. Without him, Dani lost his closest companion....

But will it really matter anymore? After all, Lia and I are running away at dusk. I'll probably never see Alexi again anyway.

Dani sighed, hurrying to collect his meager belongings. He needed to get out of here and find some way to provision this flight. His credit case was woefully thin. The coffee for breakfast had almost cleaned him out.

He hadn't worried at the time, because he didn't need credits to go alone, but with Lia... *Where can I get more credits—fast?*

He glanced at the small pile of possessions lying on the bunk. Nothing of much value: a comb, a letter of

35

commendation, a couple of medals he couldn't yet bring himself to part with, the glass ornament picked up on that first disastrous raid and kept as a kind of penance... The only other things he owned were the clothes on his back and the blanket on his bunk. The army owed him three months' back pay, but he guessed he'd better not hold his breath for that.

With a shrug, he bundled his possessions in his blanket.

"You there!"

Dani whirled—tensed to spring—and relaxed when he recognized Alexi. "Am I glad to see you, Alexi! I need to ask you some questions, and... I wanted a chance to say goodbye—"

"What are you doing there?" The grim voice bore no resemblance to Alexi's usual breezy cheerfulness. "These quarters are for military personnel only."

Dani glanced down at his worn uniform and then back at Alexi. "Technically, I guess I still qualify. Alexi, listen—"

"I don't know where you stole that uniform, or how you know my name, but I intend to find out." Alexi lifted his rifle. "Come with me."

"Alexi, it's me... Dani—"

"I've never seen you before in my life," Alexi replied harshly. "Now move."

Dani's heart sank. His worst fears proved true—the Desensitizer had changed Alexi from a happy-go-lucky draftee counting the days till release to a grim mercenary with the flip of a switch. So much for "I'll talk to him."

36

Alexi had been the only hope Dani had left in camp. The only possible source of information and maybe a few credits. Now, who could say?

Dani gathered up his blanket. At least he'd be prepared when he had the chance to slip loose from Alexi. And the chance *would* come. It had to.

***

Lia followed the stranger through the hot sunlit streets without a single thought except that her father was in trouble. All plans to run away with Dani were shoved to the corners of her consciousness by the overwhelming prayer—*Let Papa be all right*. The slim figure in front of her moved quickly and efficiently through the maze of the central market square, easy to spot in his crisp, green uniform.

Lia wanted to ask what had happened, where was her father, any of a hundred questions, but he hurried onward, confident that she still followed him. Finally, she could take no more. "What kind of accident was it?" she asked breathlessly. "Where is Papa?"

He glanced back over his shoulder briefly. "We're almost there, Miss. They will answer all your questions when we arrive."

Where was "there?" She gazed around her curiously. This part of the city was unfamiliar to her. Buildings gleamed with the raw look of fresh concrete before the inevitable patina of grime had clogged up its pores. This was new growth and miles from her side of town. She would have a difficult time getting home without her escort...

The soldier had stopped before a squat building with a windowless facade. He opened the door politely and gestured inside. "In here, Miss."

Lia hung back. "This isn't a hospital—or even a clinic. If Papa's hurt, why would they bring him here?"

"Just step inside, Miss." There was a trace of irritation in the smooth voice, the first emotion she'd heard from him.

"I think I'd better go home," she murmured, beginning to back away slowly.

The soldier drew a pistol. "I really think it would be better if you didn't try that," he snarled, the polite mask discarded. "Get inside."

Lia's eyes widened and her mind swiftly weighed the pros and cons of flight. She decided she could never hope to outrun a bullet, so stepped past him into the dimly lit interior.

He followed; the pistol held level with the middle of her back. She could feel it behind her as surely as if it actually touched her. "Answer just one question," she murmured softly. "Is my father all right?"

"I wouldn't know," he replied. "I've never met him."

"It was all a lie?"

"Think of that as the bright side."

Lia seethed at her own gullibility—she should have asked questions, demanded proof... something!

Instead, I blindly followed a stranger merely because he told me to. What will Papa say? And Dani will think I am still a child!

38

Dani... Does this soldier have something to do with Dani...?

"Why have you brought me here?"

"The General will explain."

"Why would the General want to see me?"

"Save the questions." He shoved her through an open doorway and she barely kept her feet. When she'd recovered her balance, Lia looked round the room she found herself in. It was large and rectangular, empty except for an oversized desk and chair with the flag of the Consolidation hanging behind it.

The top of the desk was clear except for a pen and pencil set placed precisely in the center of the leading edge. Before the desk stood the most important man in the Consolidation, General Merisford Cardikof.

Despite the nominal leadership of the Consolidation Governors, everyone knew that the true power in the world lay with Cardikof. After all—his efforts had almost single-handedly ended the War. His suggestions were sure to find their way into laws without opposition. In fact, a gratified Board of Governors had offered to make him King of the Global Consolidation—twice.

The great man had modestly declined, of course— he knew the real power to lie on the fringes of the government. Instead he had accepted the post as head of the Unified Armies and issued his edict. All soldiers would submit to the De-Sensitize Process for "their own good," or face court-martial and interment. There had been no provisions for individual circumstances.

But if Dani doesn't want the treatment, I'll stick by him. And if that means we run, we run.

Caught up in her own thoughts, Lia was startled to realize the general was speaking to her and she hadn't heard a word he said. "Forgive me, sir... I was concerned about my father. They said he had been in an accident?"

"No problem at all, my dear." He snapped his fingers. Her guide rolled in a fine leather chair and placed it before the desk. "Thank you, Frezon."

The man nodded curtly and started from the room.

"Oh, and Frezon..." the general purred.

"Yes, sir?" There was a trace of anxiety in the man's voice.

Lia frowned. What is he afraid of?

"It was unfortunate how Miss Vaire almost fell entering the office. Please check and make sure there is no trip hazard in the doorway. We wouldn't want the incident repeated."

"No, sir," mumbled the soldier, his face white as paper. "It won't happen again, sir."

A threat was just made and received, Lia mused, without a word of it being spoken.... This is a powerful man indeed.

"Please, sit." The general gestured toward the chair Lia perched on the edge of it, her hands laced on the top of the desk. "I was told my father was hurt, sir. Is this true?"

"I'm sorry, my dear. There seems to have been some kind of an error. I told Frezon I had something of importance to discuss with you, but no mention was made of your father at all. He must have misunderstood my request. I will have to speak to him about that."

Something in the man's tone sent a chill through her and Lia shivered. "No, I'm sure it was an honest mistake. Please don't bother on my account. What did you wish to speak to me about?"

The general moved to sit behind the desk, steepling his fingers under his chin as he leaned toward her. "I believe you are acquainted with one of my men, a Captain Zenov."

Dani is a captain? Lia felt a thrill of pride run through her. It was an honorable rank for a foot soldier to attain. "Yes, I know him." She twisted the engagement ring on her finger nervously. "He's my fiancé." It was the first time she had said it out loud. *It feels good.*

"Really? Congratulations, my dear. He is a lucky man indeed."

Lia felt her cheeks reddening. "Thank you," she murmured. "What is it that you want from me?"

"Have you heard of the Desensitizer Edict?"

"Of course."

"Have you discussed it with Captain Zenov?"

"Briefly."

"Did he tell you that he has refused the treatment?"

"Yes. He is afraid it will change his personality."

"And what did you tell him about this fear?"

"I told him that I thought he was wrong, but it was ultimately his decision and I would stand by him, whatever his final choice might be."

The general shook his head with a sad little smile. "Ah, my dear. You are only fueling his delusion. His compliance is for the good of the entire

41

Alliance. Zenov is one of a handful of holdouts. As long as he continues to refuse the treatment, the public will question why. And I would rather that not happen."

"I don't understand. Why should anyone care what Dani does or doesn't do? Surely a captain is not so important in the grand scheme of things."

"It's his importance as a symbol that I am concerned about, my dear." The general studied a sheaf of papers he retrieved from the desk drawer. "My sources say that there are those among the populace that consider the Desensitizer to be an instrument of the devil. They have the mistaken idea that its use will somehow diminish them as individuals. This belief was waning as they saw the soldiers eagerly embracing the treatment... until Zenov refused to submit. Now they are beginning to question again. I can't have that."

"We'll go away. No one needs to know that Dani hasn't undergone the procedure."

"I'm afraid that won't be good enough. I'm sure you can understand my position." He rose to his feet and came to lean against the desk before her. "You are my bargaining chip. He will do it for you."

Lia stared up at him. "What are you saying?"

Cardikof reached down and cupped her chin in his hand, lifting her head. Lia felt her soul contract at the touch. The general's eyes were flat yet hungry as his glance raked down her body. "I think any man with a pulse would do anything you asked."

She tried to pull free of his grasp, but his fingers tightened with bruising force. She gulped. "I won't force him."

"I didn't intend to give you a choice, my dear." The general's voice was smooth and cold. She felt as if ice water were being poured into her veins.

What can I do? How can I warn Dani? He won't know where I am. He won't understand...he'll believe them....

"I won't help you," she reiterated.

"That is too bad. You are such a pretty girl." He shrugged. "But it is unimportant. All that is important is that he believes you desire him to cooperate. When he finds out the truth, it will be too late. And he will no longer care." He jerked her to her feet by the jaw.

Lia was thrown off balance by the movement, falling forward into him. His other arm tightened around her waist and he pulled her into him. She could feel the hard, muscular lines of his body beneath his uniform.

The arm around her waist slipped lower and he ground his hips against hers. Lia struggled against him. Her heart pounded in terror.

He bared his teeth in a mirthless smile. "You are a little innocent, aren't you? Did you save yourself all these years for your knight in shining armor? Isn't it a letdown to find that armor tarnished? To see him hold his own well-being above that of the entire population? Do you think he cares one jot for you, you silly little fool?"

Lia forced the words past her dry throat with difficulty. "Dani loves me. Dani has always loved me."

She felt his hand groping beneath her skirt and raked her nails across his face.

43

With an outraged oath, he swung her around and pinned her against the desk, bending her backwards until she must collapse or her spine would snap. Lia continued to struggle, but he was much stronger than she.

Sobs of disgust and terror wracked her as he fumbled free of his uniform and tore aside her skirt. She felt a hard, hot bar against her thigh and then an agonizing pain as he shoved himself to the hilt within her, ripping through all barriers. Lia screamed and the general laughed like a madman.

He continued to rut inside her, his thrusts growing harder and faster. Lia sobbed like a child. *Dani will hate me. He will never forgive me. I didn't fight hard enough. I have betrayed his trust. Oh, God! What will become of me now?*

Suddenly, the general stiffened then ground his hips one last fraction tighter against her. She felt a rush of hot liquid inside her and something within her died.

Cardikof pumped his hips once or twice more then slid out of her. His eyes glittered and a cruel smile twisted his lips. "No one's little virgin now. Tsk, tsk… what will your precious Dani say to that? But you won't care. No, no, my dear. You fit me well. I think I'll keep you for myself. At least until I tire of you."

The tears that pooled in her eyes and spilt upon the desktop blurred Lia's vision, making his face a grotesque mask. "What will you do to me?" she whispered, her heart broken beyond repair.

44

"I'll soon make you forget that you've ever even dreamed of anyone but me." He stepped back and adjusted his clothes.

Lia lay across the desk, too wounded in body and soul to move.

He grabbed her wrist and dragged her from the office. She stumbled after him, her thoughts whirling like leaves in a millrace. What will Dani think of me? I'm dirty and used... broken. How will he be able to love me after this? I tried so hard. I waited so long. He will hate me! Dani will hate me....

Her mind kept repeating the same thought over and over again, as the tears streamed down her face.

***

Alexi kept his rifle pointed squarely in the center of Dani's back. Dani could feel it there as surely as if it touched his spine. His gaze darted from side to side, searching for an opening—for some opportunity to break away from his former friend.

That's what hurts the most. Alexi was the only real friend I had in the entire United Forces. Why did they have to send him? Is it part of the plan to break me? Why can't they leave me in peace? Why is a single man such a threat to the United Forces? All I want is a little hut somewhere with Lia at my side... maybe a garden. I am so tired of war. Why won't they leave me in peace?

Dani was preoccupied by his thoughts and was shaken out of his reverie when Alexi slammed the barrel of his rifle home between Dani's shoulder blades. "In there, Zenov." He jerked his head toward a concrete Quonset hut set on a square of bare earth.

Dani stepped through the doorway, blinking to adjust his eyes to the dim interior after the late afternoon sunlight. A corridor stretched to either side of him and a doorway stood immediately opposite. He hesitated over which way to go, Dani received another shove from Alexi's rifle barrel. "In there."

Dani stumbled through the doorway into a nearly empty office. His eyes were still adjusting to the change of light, but he could see the figure seated behind the desk and his heart grew cold. He forced himself to remain calm, snapped to attention, hand going to his forehead in formal salute. "General Cardikof, sir."

The general leaned forward on his desk. "I don't think there is any reason to pretend you still consider yourself a soldier, Zenov." The words were cold. "I know that you were planning to desert rather than follow orders. Did you really think that I would not find out?"

Dani lowered his hand to his side, clenching his fists to hide his trembling. "What do you mean, sir?"

"Your little plan has been discovered. You might as well submit to the inevitable now. You have no reason left to hold out. Comply with the edict and you will retain your position in my army—in fact, I will see you made Major. A nice promotion, a handsome raise in pay...."

46

"All I want is to be left alone, sir." Dani could hear himself pleading, but could not stop it—despite the fact he knew it was to no avail. *I have to try. For Lia...*

And then the blow that drove him to his knees... the general held out his hand and a woman stepped out of the shadows to take it. A beautiful, doll-like face exquisitely made up, with hair coiffed to perfection. Her gown was silk and fell in graceful swirls about her sensual body. She was stunning. She looked at him in polite disinterest, her lovely eyes devoid of all emotion.

Lia didn't even recognize him.

The general reached up to fondle the underside of one of her breasts. Dani leapt forward and received a rifle butt to the temple. He staggered, dazed by the blow.

"I believe you've met my new companion," the general commented, his expression feral. "Elianora, my dear, this is Daniscar Zenov. You've heard me speak of him."

"Of course, Merisford." She held out a dainty hand, her nails perfectly manicured. "How do you do, Captain Zenov?"

Dani choked back a sob.

"She is a quick study, this one is." The general pulled Lia into his lap then gave her a long, deep kiss. His hands roamed freely up and down her body and Lia arched against him.

Dani buried his face in his hands. No... no... he has taken the last precious thing I had in this world... there is nothing left. Nothing.

47

The general broke the kiss with a satisfied sigh. "Yes, she is a marvel, this one is. Too bad you never had a chance to find that out for yourself. But then, it's never too late, is it? Lia, my dear, would you be so good as to give Captain Zenov some idea of what he is missing?"

Obediently, Lia came around the desk and stopped in front of Dani. She let the silk dress fall from her shoulders, and stood, naked to the waist. Her gaze was focused on the wall behind Dani, and there was no trace of expression in her eyes.

"You may touch her if you like," the general offered. "I certainly have."

Dani groaned low in his throat, shoulders sagging in utter defeat. *Oh, Lia... my precious girl. What have I done to you?*

He rose to his feet. Every movement was like wading through quicksand. He reached out and drew Lia's dress back onto her shoulders. For a heartbeat, he let his hand linger on her cheek and she smiled. His breath caught in his throat then he realized the vapid smile did not reach her eyes. *She doesn't know me. She doesn't know me at all.*

"See what a marvelous job the Desensitizer can do, Zenov? Look at your friend, Alexi—the perfect soldier. Look at Elianora—the perfect mistress. You, my friend... you could be the perfect commander. You have intelligence; you learn quickly you adapt well. Without your crushing emotional hang-ups, you would be invincible. Join me and I will even give you back your lovely lady. The two of you can live happily ever *new* after. What do you say?"

48

Dani looked from General Cardikof to Lia. We will be strangers. She may never love me again...but I cannot bear this pain. He's won at last.

Squaring his shoulders, Dani took a deep breath. "Drink my soul... please."

Brighton Baroque (Liam A. Spinage)

A gull wheels across the sky at sunset, keen eyes surveying the surf. Unlike its compatriots, it is not seeking sustenance. This gull has a mission. It dips its ink-tipped wings and dives, dives, dives. Over the entrance to the chain pier, causing considerable consternation among the pedestrians populating the promenade. Over the Victoria fountain with its stone dolphins. It rests briefly on the lip of a balustrade on the Royal Pavilion, not so much as to get its bearings as to gather its thoughts. Will they remember the ancient compact? Will they honour it, as their mother and father would have wished? Will they be of suitable character and bearing to deal with the resurgent menace?

It scratches its beak against a wing - it is unused to such complicated thoughts and doesn't really want them - it flaps down to the Theatre Royal opposite and raps politely on a small window to the left of the stage door. Then it paces back and forth, pecking occasionally at the fine film of dust while it waits for a reply.

Beyond that window in a stuffy, undersized dressing room, two figures argue in raised but perfectly formed voices.

"Clementine, dear heart, please be sparing with the foundation. We haven't a lot left." The voice is clear, somewhat shrill in indignation and loud enough to be heard in any of the dressing rooms, though not on the stage.

"Oh Clement, joy of my life, please do shut your perpetually whingeing cakehole and pass me my moustache." This voice is deeper, heartier somehow, but no less sonorous.

There is a knock at the door - fragile, unsure - and it opens slightly. A nervous figure enters with a tray.

"Champagne for you both. And chocolates." He indicates a small box stuffed with peppermint creams fashioned to resemble miniature seashells.

"Well, that's thoughtful. Isn't that thoughtful, sister of mine?"

The gull looks on nervously, trying to peek through the thick layer of grime. It hops back and forth for a few moments, making sure it has the right window, and taps again, furiously. If these two are meant to save the day, then the day is in a lot of trouble. Not to mention tomorrow.

Finally, the window creaks open ever so slightly, enough for it to stick its head through and fully inspect the appointed saviours of the town. As it does, it is met with a shriek of horror which only a trained actor could muster.

"Shoo! Get away, wretched vermin!" A procession of objects, ever increasing in size and hardness, are catapulted in its direction. It dodges deftly, then re-alights on the sill and - in a welcome interlude to the harassment - scratches with its beak in the dirt.

"IT HAS RETURNED."

Both the humans in the room change their demeanour rapidly. They invite it inside; even prepare it a cushion, now they're aware of what it is.

51

Not just a gull. A harbinger of ill omen. A message from beyond the grave, somehow - from their own dear father, departed sadly these 22 years. This is the day they were warned about. A day they have been preparing for. Just not one they had expected to interrupt their three-week star billing at the Theatre Royal.

"Clementine, sister dearest?"
"Yes, brother of mine?"
"It's time to get things started." Clementine was already removing some of the more obvious elements of her outfit - the top hat, the glue-on moustache, the outlandish monocle that gave her stage gentleman-persona that air of distinction.
Clement had a much longer job of it. He was still removing layers of crinoline, bustle and silk bloomers as his sister watched in what would have been taken for impatience had it not been punctuated with occasional mirthfulness. Finally, in a last act of exasperation, he clutched at his pearls and declared. "Oh, do help me, sister of mine. It's one thing to be seen in this on the stage, it's quite another to wear it on the street, let alone when we are about Society business!"
Clementine reached over, snatching her brother's hands together imperiously and commanding him to stand still while she disengaged him from masses of female undergarments. When she was done, Clement pecked her on the cheek by means of thanks.
"Where would I be without you? Now, where's our avian visitor gone?"

"He's behind you."

The two of them turned round together and regarded the gull with utmost seriousness.

"Can it talk, do you think?"

"Not so, brother dear, not so. It is a mere messenger. A warning that another threat from the sea has come. We must act swiftly to determine the nature of the menace. Are you ready to travel?"

"As good as I can be. Besides, nobody will really notice in the dark. We're bound to attract some attention, but we've carefully cultivated an air of eccentricity that will serve us well. Ready when you are!"

At that, they left their dressing room and made their way to the stage door, evading angry glances from both stagehands and their producer. The show must go on, but tonight it was a different show.

Back in the dressing room, the lone gull looked up wearily, grabbed one of the elegantly wrapped chocolate shells in its beak and flew back out of the window, high and away into the night air.

***

Clementine June Weatherlie and Clement August Weatherlie made their way from the stage door through the dingy alley at the back of the theatre and ran briskly across the road, lest they be recognised by the crowd outside the door who had come to see them perform. This managed, Clementine took a key from her reticule while her brother looked over his shoulder ready to fend off any autograph hunters. The key fitted perfectly into a little-known door in the grounds of the Pavilion, a door that had not seen much use since the death of their father in the great storm of 1850. They were entering the local archives of the Aletheian Society - masses of parchments, tomes, objects d'art and occult paraphernalia meticulously collected by the previous generations who had served in the Society - including their dear departed father - and equally meticulously catalogued and maintained by their erstwhile personages. While they had dealt with all manner of supernatural threats in their time, they had been ultimately preparing for what they called The Threat From The Sea (they both agreed it was worthy of capitalisation) - the very threat that had caused the great storm and taken their father from them too soon.

"Father's notes are quite clear on this, as you are aware."

Clement nodded in reply. "It would do us good to have a last review of them, I think, before we execute the plan of action."

"Agreed. Please be so kind, brother dear, to pass me 'The Book of All The Ancient Customs' and father's notes."

Clement fumbled at the latch of a cabinet, his hands shaking slightly, and opened it to reveal a treasure of terrible tomes. He reached for a weighty volume which had the singular pleasure of its own shelf and looked at the catch, fashioned to resemble two dolphins chasing each other.

The book set firmly on the table, Clementine opened it with tremulous hands and wondrous eyes. Here was the prize of their collection: the tome which bore the ancient compact between the fisherfolk of the shore and the townsfolk who had arrived later. Two copies of this tome existed - one for each party - and it was a matter of some consternation that the twins did not know which copy they had or how their father - on behalf of the Society - had come to procure it.

The volume itself was old - as old as the town of Brighthelmston - and the hinged dolphins gave way creakily to reveal the text inside. The contents were familiar to the twins, who had pored over it a thousand times in preparation for this day: how the townsfolk and the fisherfolk had banded together to rid the ancient town of the first menace from the sea, carefully annotated illustrations of its malevolent form and how to defeat it when it rose again. Of central concern in the appendices to the tome penned by their father was the following passage about how the threat became manifest:

"There has always been perceived among those who dwell on the coast a danger from the ocean that those who live inland cannot understand, whether from onshore storm, flooding or malevolent aquatic fauna. Periodically, unknown triggers bring forth what I am forced to conclude is a manifestation of the collected consciousness made flesh; an enemy that can be fought and, one must hope, vanquished. This has been so since the first stories of knuckers in waterholes and talk of dragons in Ethelward's Chronicles."

"So," muttered Clement, "are we to be gallant knights-errant and slay the beast with weapons? Or are we going to be more like the cunning Jim Pulk and bake it a poison pie? I confess my skills at either are somewhat lacking."

"Wits, I think, win the day," replied Clementine, "At least that would be my preference. Also, given the cyclical nature of attack and defence that father noted, I suspect we will have to face that poison ourselves - though in what manner I find hard to deduce - and should thus be prepared."

"Oh, joys," quipped Clement. "Can it be a surfeit of champagne? At least then I can die happily."

"Hush! No talk of dying, please, brother dearest. I think we need to bring this matter to the attention of the third member of our little circle and see what he has to say."

Clement harrumphed. "He never seems to say anything of import. But lead on!"

"Well, let's be away then and see what wisdom he's in the mood to dispense today."

***

Namrik had technically been a member of the Aletheian Society for fifty-two years, which would have made him one of the Society's longest-serving members were he actually a human being. Instead - its consciousness being a result of a wishing lamp being accidentally soldered on to one of Charles Babbage's prototype computational contraptions - Namrik was forced to eke out a meagre existence as a fortune telling machine beneath the chain pier; a favourite among the weekend crowd but a pale imitation of an unfulfilled destiny. The twins had first been introduced to him by their parents when they were young; it was only in discussion with the elders of the Aletheian Society that Namrik's true history had come to the fore. It remained a mystery to Clement why the Society placed more stock in this machine than the abilities of their human agents. It was less of a mystery to Clementine, who was currently wondering why Clement was only wearing one shoe.

Clement fumbled in his pocket for a shilling and inserted it wearily into the slot. Namrik sprang into life, the cogs and wheels clicking and computing as the automaton's piercing blue eyes searched for the image of who had deigned to disturb him. Some two minutes later, after a not inconsiderable amount of jerky hand-waving beneath ill-tailored silk sleeves, the machine spat out a token. Clement withdrew it from the machine and looked it over.

YOU WILL MEET A TALL DARK STRANGER

Clement sighed.

"Let me try," muttered Clementine. "Pass me a shilling, darling brother of mine." Namrik's eyes glowed blue momentarily - had they ever done that before? she wondered - and there followed a long period of silence interrupted only by a series of clacks and whirrs until, eventually, his wisdom spent, Namrik spat out a second token which she turned over in her hand. Upon it there were no words, merely a picture of a shell. For a moment, she was one of mind with her brother.

"I've seen that before!" Clement exclaimed, tugging on her sleeve. "Somewhere recently…"

"Oh, do think clearly!" Clementine held her brother's hands in hers as she implored him to remember.

"In the tome! Wait, no, in father's notes! It's an ammonite!"

"Of course! It's a facsimile of a fossil, not anything current. The architect Amon Wilds decorated buildings with them all over the city, as a play on his name. And he was father's chief suspect, he accused Wilds of using his architecture as a geomantic summoning grid writ large over the whole town! That must be what Namrik is trying to tell us!"

"Wilds must be dead by now though, surely?" Clementine resisted the urge to slap her sibling. They should both be aware by now that things didn't always stay dead. Especially after that incident on the promenade last summer. Luckily, he corrected himself with an 'Oh,' and then tailed off.

"He died in 1833, brother dear, suspiciously only a few days after the collapse of the Anthaeum. It was the architecture not the architect that father suspected."

Clement straightened himself. "Well, nothing a few blows with a pickaxe won't cure, then! We can smash those shells and be done in one night!"

"We will need that pickaxe, that's true. Also maybe a shovel. Brother dear, we need to raise the dead."

***

"The trouble with the dead," Clement mused as he wiped sweat from his brow. "Is that they should

58

stay dead." He paused for a moment, leaning on the pickaxe in the ill-lit graveyard on top of the hill. It was trivial enough to find the architect's grave - there was a bloody great ammonite on it - but digging it up was hard work, especially as Clementine had insisted he did the work alone while she 'kept vigil.'

They had made their way to the rear of the churchyard undisturbed - it was past midnight now, they thought. The only person they had seen in the vicinity was a tall man dressed in an impeccable dark blue suit and matching top hat, who seemed quite unaware of their presence and was content to stare intently into the night sky, softly calling, as they crept past.

Now, though, as she stood shivering, Clementine became acutely aware that they were being watched - by someone or something - and it gave her chills beyond that of a dark summer's night.

"Are you done yet?" She inquired over her shoulder.

Clement grunted in reply.

Then it came. A pair of glowing green eyes descending at them from the heavens and with it a vicious looking beak and long, white wings locked in a silent swoop.

"Aagh! Get away!"

Alerted by his sister's cry, Clement wasted no time in scrabbling from the half-dug grave to stand next to her, pickaxe at the ready, as Clementine removed a talisman from her reticule and flashed it before them in a series of rapid movements.

The gull dove again, but this time appeared to bounce off an impenetrable, invisible barrier and waddled away, stunned and reeling.

"I say! That was a rather good trick!"

It only works once. Quick, let us find some cover."

"They're not normally that vicious!"

"Yes they are! What they aren't - normally - is nocturnal. Or possessed." Clementine ducked behind a tomb as the gull took off.

"Oh." Clement flailed at it with the pickaxe as it dived toward him.

"We need to get out of here, something is very wrong..."

"You're telling me! Possessed seagulls!? Whatever next!"

"Possessed actors? That's the same seagull that warned us in our dressing room." She dived behind a tombstone as the screeching began again. The gull wheeled in an arc across the night sky, biding its time.

"Huh?"

"The ammonite shape, we've seen that before."

"I know, it's..."

"Not in father's notes! In the dressing room. It's the same shape as the chocolates that were delivered to us."

Clement tripped and sank to his muddied knees; Clementine swung back and helped him up.

"The gull has parts of the green wrapper stuck on its beak."

Clement looked aghast. "I confess I didn't look that closely..."

"Run! Now!"

The two of them leapt out of cover and high-tailed it into what they hoped was the relative protection of the church. Momentarily safe, they gasped to recover both their breath and their wits.

"So, you think the chocolates were poisoned?"

"I believe them to be part of Namrik's warning. As dangers from the sea go, though…" Clementine peered out from under the porch toward the sky. "I'll take a gull over a shark. But we need to get back, first to the theatre to inspect the chocolates and then back to the archives for their safekeeping."

"You don't think the cast have…" Clement tailed off.

"Thinks, oh joy of my existence, when was the last time you helped yourself to something unattended in a dressing room?"

"Oh Lord! We must make all haste!"

"Exactly."

The twins made short work of the journey back to the theatre, but the scene that greeted them was not what they expected. They entered through the stage door, ever alert, they had expected to encounter an entire cast of show-stopping actors with glowing eyes of emerald green. What they found instead, daubed on the walls in blue paint, was a series of glyphs that rendered them insensible. Both succumbed to the mind-numbing drowsiness the graffiti induced in them, collapsing first to their knees and then giving in to the oblivion of sleep. Whatever had chosen to menace them this night, it would appear its tactics had changed.

***

Silence. Near darkness. Only a dim twinkling from overhead, a reflection from the moon outside through layers of expensive glass.

Clementine struggled with her bonds, so she called out to her brother.

"Clement, are you there?"

"Present, sister dearest."

"Where the Dickens are we, do you imagine?"

"We're in the Regent's Saloon, inside the Pavilion."

Clementine looked over, quizzically.

"I recognise the outline of the chandelier and this particular carpet stain."

Quite how her brother was intimately familiar with the interior decor of the ballroom could wait for another day.

"Help me out, would you? I can just about reach my knife, if you loosen my rope a little…"

"Enough." A booming voice echoed throughout the room, quelling all attempts at escape.

"You will answer for your crime."

"Pray, what crime might that be?" Clementine replied sweetly, with only a tiny hint of sarcasm. "And while we're on the subject, since when do trials take place in the dead of night in formerly-royal apartments?"

"Since Queen Victoria was persuaded to relinquish the Pavilion to us, The Society of Twelve."

Clementine hadn't actually been expecting an answer; but if she had, this was the answer she would have wanted.

"Free us and show yourselves! I believe we can come to an accord against the return of true evil to

62

our beloved town. I say to you now, whose sacred societal name is known to me, that we are not your enemies."

There followed a series of hushed, frenzied whispers and the same voice spoke.

"Very well. We will show ourselves."

A flickering of light; the flare of a lantern. Then, the Society revealed their true forms to the horror of their still-bound prisoners.

***

Had Clementine still been wearing her monocle, it would at this point have fallen comically from her face at the sight before them.

She looked over at her brother. Clement, for his part, was clutching his fist in his mouth in a semblance of fear. Though it was just possible, she thought, that he was doing it to stifle a giggle.

"We are, as you can see, naturists."

One must assume that the sight of the twelve society members in their altogether was used predominantly as a shock tactic. On this occasion, it had been found wanting. There was an awkward pause measured only by the uncomfortable shuffling of feet. Clementine, who had seen more semi- or unclothed persons in her theatrical career than she cared to think about, merely blinked and then retorted.

"And we, as you can see, are cross-dressing thespian twins. We are also the representatives of the Aletheian Society in Brighton, sworn by sacred duty to protect the realm of her majesty from

63

supernatural incursions and malignant otherworldly artefacts."

"The Leafy Urn Society?" The same voice boomed, but with a mouth behind it this time; a mouth attached to a face and a naked body which was somehow glowing now with its own cerulean light. "Never heard of you."

"What gives you the right to hold secret court over our fates?" This new outburst came from Clement, still struggling with the ropes. "From what sacristy do you proclaim dominion over the unseen and unworldly, as we do?"

"By ancient compact, we protect this town from monstrous incursions from the ocean," the voice intoned. Clementine could make out more of the form attached to that voice now as it shuffled slowly forward. A thin, translucent man, but a man, nonetheless. He trailed behind him some contraption which seemed to be affixed to the rear of his neck and upper arms by lengths of translucent tubing, through which ran a clear liquid. What fresh madness was this?

"Inter Undes et Colles Floremus." The intonation echoed through the superb acoustics of the Regent's Saloon.

"What's he saying?" Clement was frantic now. "What's he SUMMONING?" He was nearly free of the ropes with all the frenzied struggling, but his sister had stayed unflinching, still bound...

"Hush, brother dearest. That's the town motto."

"By the Book Of All The Ancient Customs of the Toune of Brighthelmston, we are bound to protect the coast from the dangers of the sea."

Clementine wasn't going to question where he'd produced the book from. There were some things that were best left unquestioned. As he drew closer, his full visage became visible by the lantern light and its own eerie inner glow; gaunt, haggard and speckled with liver spots, the vestige of a grey beard trailing to his neck; beneath it, barely visible, a recognisable form in amber at his throat. An ammonite.

For the first time in this sorry affair, Clementine gasped.

"You're him! You're Amon Wilds!"

"Indeed, young woman. And I am, as you can see, neither dead nor buried."

Clement, who had wrestled free from bondage at last, rose and turned to look at the ancient man now all but hunched over his sister. Whatever he was about to do, he had better do it quickly. Wilds raised the book in his hand, however, he found himself commenting rather than confronting.

"Oh! The Book of Customs! We have one of those in the basement, don't we, Clementine my heart?"

Clementine sighed. All their cards were revealed, all the tension had left the situation. The other eleven members were at first intensely shocked at this news, then mollified.

"If that is so, then you are the partners we hoped for." Wilds spoke for them all. "Let us speak further."

***

65

"Father was convinced it was you." They had all settled in now like old friends, taking sips in Fitzherbert's after hours. "Said the ammonites gave you away. The exact form that was needed to summon creatures from the depths."

"Such an object, once used for one purpose, can be more easily diverted to the opposite. The ammonite architecture protects us all now - to some extent - by the principles of sacred geometry. Safe enough for most of us, but not her royal personage, which is why she was advised to vacate the Pavilion and leave the building to us." He added a brief afterthought. "And I keep myself alive, as it were, by having the life-giving seawaters of Brighton running through my veins rather than blood."

"How is it you have a copy of our book?" interjected Clement, sour at being left out of the discussion.

"When the customs were first scribed down, two copies were made. One remained in the town in a chest secured by three locks, which has been guarded by the Dippers on behalf of the Twelve ever since. We did not know what happened to the other."

"Somehow it either fell into father's hands and he was recruited by the Aletheian Society, or he was already a member and procured it," finished Clementine, quaffing back another tot of gin. "We may never know.,."

"You must return it to the fisherfolk in the morning. That much is imperative. We will take care of your cast until the work is done. I'm sure it won't be the first time some of them have spent the night in the cells." Wilds was thoughtful. "Do you think our plan will work? Are you prepared to enact it?"

"We will need to rest first. But yes, we'll do it."

"Then we will see you there, in Pool Valley, to lend our aid."

It had not escaped the twins' notice that this was exactly where their father had died.

***

Dawn is a taxing time of day; more so when one has only had three hours' sleep at most. Clement rubbed his eyes and groaned, standing behind his sister on the mist-laden beach, chill with morning air.

Clementine stood in conversation with three fishermen, pipes lit and arms folded. She repeated the words Wilds had taught her to say. "By ancient compact, we claim our rights to one twelfth of all your sardines." Eyebrows were raised, and one among them stepped forward.

"You are new. You are from them?"

"We are from … another … it's complicated. We're working with them, but we are also the ones in possession of your tome." She snapped her fingers and Clement moved forward at the cue, nearly tripping on the unstable shingle. He handed it over. They spoke among themselves for a few moments in a strange cant Clementine couldn't make out.

"It's back. We have a plan to take it out, but we need your consent and your control over the tome to be restored." Clementine took the initiative in the dialogue, as she usually did, before her brother began tripping over his own words.

67

"And a few fishing nets would be good, maybe a harpoon or two." Clement was impatient, shivering.

"Aye, we've sensed its approach. Storm clouds have been gathering for days. Do we go now?"

"Just to Pool Valley. We can use its unique position as the underground confluence of the Wellesbourne and the Westerbourne streams to imprison its physical form, but it won't go easily." Clementine had been impressed with the scale of Wilds' plan. From the Aquarium to the new Goldstone pumping station, it seemed that all the recent construction in Brighton had been designed for this specific purpose.

The fisherman nodded, then turned and shouted to the others who were busy preparing their nets. Clement stood alongside his sister; his neck crooked as he eavesdropped on whatever it was the fisherfolk now began saying amongst each other in their strange, shared language.

"They've agreed to it then! Good." Clementine turned, quizzically.

"You understand their cant? Brother dear, you do amaze me!"

"Sister of mine, that is Polari. It's used by fishmongers and queens both. I can understand every word of it. Shall we go?"

The twins walked grimly, hand in hand, to the place of confrontation, trailed by a dozen hardy fisherfolk with a host of barbed weapons.

***

68

Whatever they had expected at Pool Valley, it certainly wasn't nothing. In the dim glow of the dawn, the twins and their allies surveyed the scene. No storm, no flooding, no menace. One of the shops was open, however, which was certainly strange at this time. Clement nudged his sister.

"'Edmunds Chocolates.' Must be the place." As if at their bidding, a thin frame appeared at the doorway, human but barely so, eyes lit with a blazing emerald green. One harpoon flew over their head and clattered harmlessly to the floor at its feet. Enraged, it let out an unearthly screech and dropped to all fours.

"Now!" shouted Clement. Two of the Society of Twelve, marked as their 'Dipper' guards by their elegant bathing costumes, struggled with the manholes to the drains as the fishers began to encircle the enemy.

It grew in size, audibly popping joints and letting out howls as it did so. Clouds began to gather overhead, blotting out the sun, and then it started to rain. The scaled monstrosity that now gibbered and writhed before them struck out with a savage claw, rending one brave fisherman in half.

"Westerbourne, now!" Clementine roared the order, struggling now to be heard above the torrential rain. There was a great clunk and the drain gushed forth its load; fresh water to add to the rain. The creature hesitated slightly, spinning its slavering jaws in torment.

"Wellesbourne!" The second drain opened; the swell of the Wellesbourne spreading from the drain at the opposite side of the courtyard.

"Clementine! It's working!" Wilds, surveying from above, shouted. "But it's not enough! Dam the coastal barrage, that will divert the flows! Both water sources must be in full flow for the scheme to have effect!"

The twins cursed as the creature shrugged off attack after attack. The water was ankle deep now as they sloshed their way toward the promenade, deftly avoiding tooth and claw alike in their struggle. The Twelve had nearly finished the barrage, just a few sandbags left…

The draconic form writhed and twisted, held down now by nets and constrained by the fresh water flushing the poison from its mind and body. It lashed furiously over and over again, gibbering, howling, the light dying within it until it was no more than a shell of itself.

Clementine paused for a breath. "It's done."

Wilds approached, dragging his brine tank behind him. "It is over. We can take it from here. We thank the Aletheian Society for its valuable assistance."

Clementine nodded. "If you ever need us again, you know where we are. Although don't try and enter without permission. There will be consequences."

"I might say the same of us. Still, there is no reason not to be cordial."

"Quite." Clementine turned to her brother. "We're on stage in three hours. Ready for it?"

"After this?" grinned Clement. "Child's play!" He sauntered off toward the Pavilion loudly singing a bawdy ditty. Clementine, with a sigh and a smile, followed him.

Jiangshi (David Turnbull)

Mao had once said, quoting the philosopher Lau Tzu, that a journey of a thousand miles begins with a single step. That being the case, Han wondered how many thousands of miles he had journeyed since he'd taken his first step. How many steps had he accumulated since the Long March ended the civil war in China and set in train the Great March Forward of the Red Army into Nepal and Korea and Mongolia? How many miles had been marched since the column he was assigned to cross into North Africa?

He squinted against the rays of the morning sun and watched the Commissar climb onto a munitions box to deliver the daily *thought*. She was short and could not be seen at the back of the massed ranks of the battalions. But her voice was loud and she had the aid of a megaphone. She was also multilingual and so could deliver the *thought* in the half dozen mother tongues of the conscripted soldiers gathered before her in the bright coastal sun of the North African dawn.

"When faced with seemingly insurmountable adversity," she pronounced, "a true revolutionary regards the situation within the context of the greater struggle. And, in doing so, is prepared both mentally and physically for what is about to unfold."

The latest recruits clapped respectfully. Because that was expected of them. The clap rippled like an incoming wave as the *thought* was interpreted into

71

language after language. For Han this was like a mystical experience. Who knew how many days ago Comrade Mao had articulated this wisdom? But it had travelled via runners by word of mouth from one to the next, along the largely stationary main trunk of the Great March, out through the forward moving boughs and onward to innumerate branches and spikey off-shoots such as this one.

Han looked at the gigantic silk banners unfurled at the fringes of the assembled ranks. The Chairman's wise and benevolent image smiled down on combatants of his global insurgency. Han's heart swelled with pride. It felt as if the leader was omnipresent, radiating revolutionary fervour and optimistic positivity.

Today's words seemed incredibly apt.

Across the straits of Gibraltar, the British fleet had assembled, funnels billowing flumes of grey smoke, massed guns trained on the fallen Spanish territory of Ceuta, north of Morocco. With the metal stars on the flat caps of the battalions sparking in the sunlight and the Commissar's voice resonating in his ears, Han could feel a strong sense of destiny transitioning into history.

Soon the British bombardment would commence. It would be long and relentless. But the twelve battalions of this division of the International People's Liberation Army would disperse and regroup. As they done so many times before. Disperse and regroup. Disperse and regroup. That was the mantra of the Great March Forward. The imperialist generals of the West did not remotely grasp this method of warfare and thus were frequently routed at every skirmish or battle.

The architects of the March were experts in the art of war. They knew how to comprehensively encircle a city and hold it the vicelike stranglehold of a siege. They knew how to infiltrate its populace with spies and saboteurs and how best to swamp their meeting places with propaganda. They knew how to convert workers and soldiers to the revolutionary cause and turn them from passive initiates into active insurgents. Han had witnessed this time and again. He had seen city after city fall, like trees in a forest succumbing to the lumberjack's axe.

Of course, the decisive factor in the IPLA's unstoppable advance was the Jiangshi. It was the Jiangshi that made their class enemies tremble with fear. They, more than anything, caused armies to surrender and throw down their arms. Han could see them, off in the distance, packed into the interlocking trains of cages hooked behind the flat bed tow trucks that hauled them when the march was on the move. Blue skinned and bloated, snarling and foaming at the mouth, throwing themselves against the bars, waiting for the feeding frenzy that would ensue when the limbs and torsos of captive traitors of the counter insurgency were tossed into their midst.

Release and recapture, this was the mantra. The Jiangshi were the storm troopers of the revolution. They replenished their numbers by passing their infection on to those who foolishly attempted to halt the advance of the Great March. They, beyond anything else, were why progress was being made at such a phenomenal rate.

As consequence of their deployment the Great March continued to gather momentum, branching off in different directions, seizing territory, crawling over entire continents and smothering nations like a briar rose. Mao the beating heart. The March the arteries and veins. The Jiangshi the teeth and claws.

***

Han had been there from the start. When it had been a desperate cat and mouse retreat from the advance of Generalissimo Chiang Kai-shek and his Kuomintang nationalists. Now it was a global phenomenon. The Great March moved like a many-headed serpent, growing in length and girth as soldiers and peasants, workers and intellectuals from Seoul to Timbuktu shook off the chains of their subjugation to join its revolutionary ranks.

Their first encounter with the Jiangshi had been almost poetic.

They were marching wearily through rural China, supplies depleted, morale at a low ebb. The sun a red disc rising over a distant slate grey mountain range. Fronds of mist danced above the rice paddies. The rice grass unkempt and wild, as if the harvest was long overdue. A heron perched on a mud dyke, alighting with a squirming frog in its beak.

Then, ominous ripples breaking in the paddies, the slosh of water. As if something shrouded by the mist was rising out of the sediment and disturbing the stillness of the surface. The dawn chirrup of the crickets falling ominously silent. Mud covered figures lurching out of the miasma, eerily silhouetted by the dawn, approaching the bank in a unified but unsynchronised motion, like an uncertain dance troupe that had neglected its rehearsals.

A lone soldier waded into the paddies to greet them. "Join us, brothers," he said. "Workers and peasants united. Despite the current set back, our revolution shall not be defeated."

The figures pitched forward in juddering motion and the odd, unsettling blueness of their flesh became apparent. Han saw the how their eyeballs bulged like fat, overripe fruits, almost bursting out of their sockets beneath the sodden brims of their straw hats. He saw the hordes of black leeches that sucked on their faces and arms.

"Brothers," said the soldier. "We are the Red Army. We bring liberation and salvation. Long live the revolution."

The strange looking farmers had formed an arc before him. They stood knee deep in the paddy. Veined nostrils flared, as if they had somehow gotten scent of the week old perspiration ingrained in him from the rigours of the march. There came a low, bestial growling. Something seemed instantaneously to click within them. Their slowness quickened in that instant. Before the soldier could retreat to the bank they fell upon him like wolves, pulling him down into the muddy water, clawing with ragged fingernails, ripping the flesh from his bones with their snapping teeth.

Gunfire and confusion ensued.

Followed by a frantic tactical withdrawal.

Sharp shooters were hurriedly stationed at the crest of a small hillock. They took out the ravaging Jiangshi with headshot before they could submerge themselves once more into the paddies. In the aftermath an exploratory party was dispatched to scout out the nearest village. Han was selected and told that, as such, a great honour had been bestowed upon him.

Han didn't believe this to be the case. He suspected the scouting party was made up of those who had singularly failed to impress the military hierarchy. Han was pale skinned and skinny as a stick. His mother was a bar girl who had fallen pregnant to an American sailor. His hands had never wielded a hammer or swung a sickle. He was neither an industrial labourer, nor a son of the soil. He was dispensable.

And so, he surmised, were the others selected with him.

The village was little more than a single dirt track, ramshackle houses to one side, rice paddies to the other. Rusted, well used, farm implements hanging from iron hooks on awkwardly leaning porches. Threadbare peasant clothing fluttering on rusted wire washing lines. Abandoned cooking pots sitting on the cold ashes of dead fires.

Poor people lived here. It was the sort of village where the doctrine of the CCP would normally receive an enthusiastic reception. Where young men and women, downtrodden by grinding poverty, would be only too willing to take up arms in the revolutionary cause of the Red Army.

But the place appeared deserted.

Six of them walked the potholed dirt track that led into the village, two by two, side by side. Four men and two women. All in the shabby remnants of their Red Army uniform. Despite the morning chill, Han worried that his hands were sweating to the extent that his rifle might slip from his grip. He couldn't get the image of that poor soldier being ripped to shreds out of his head.

Jiangshi.

He'd heard the word being whispered mouth to mouth before the patrol set off. Han was a city boy, but he knew the legend. He didn't think the term was being applied properly. The creatures they'd encountered were not the hopping vampires mythologized in cautionary tales old grandmothers told about the undead. He supposed though that it was human nature to try and rationalize the unknown by giving it a name.

The village was silent. They progressed, watching for signs of life. The run-down houses to one side of them and to the other, the verdant rice grass of the paddies, eerily undulating in the breeze that had dispersed the mist.

They came upon something lying in a dark heap in the road. They drew slowly closer and then it revealed itself to be the remains of a water buffalo. It had been torn apart, belly ripped open, horned head almost severed from its bulky neck, guts strewn in the mud. Black flies hummed around it, fat creamy maggots squirming in the redness of its

77

rancid meat, little birds pecking at its shredded hide. Han touched its flank with his boot and gasped as a sleek black rat scurried out of its chest cavity and leapt for the cloudy water of the rice paddies.

Then from the garbage strewn yard of one of the houses an odd-looking brown dog appeared. Barking and growling, emaciated ribs showing beneath moulting fur, teeth bared, foaming at the mouth as if it might be rabid. It raced towards them, spindly hind legs kicking up dust. Han saw the blue of its flesh through the mangy patches of fur. He saw how it eyes bulged fat in their sockets. How its belly hung like a fat, mutated udder.

It leapt towards them and one of the comrades raised her rifle and shot it in the head. It tumbled limply through the air and came to a halt when it hit the remains of the water buffalo. The flies rose and scattered in a panicking cloud, only to reform and descend to the fresh carrion a moment later.

Han felt his heart thumping rapidly in his chest. He barely had a moment to catch his thoughts before all hell broke loose. Apparently roused by the shot, the inhabitants of the village emerged from the gloomy interiors of their hovels. The mothers and their children, the elderly and infirm, all those who had not been actively engaged in the rice harvest. Each one

infected with whatever foul epidemic had seized the village, shuffling, snarling, blue flesh, bulging eyes, grotesquely fat bellies, foaming at the mouth like the dog.

Everyone, including Han, began firing off rounds but the numbers were too great. They were coming at them from every direction. The front, the rear, the side. Even from the paddies, for it seemed not all of the marksmen had hit their marks. Soon they were backed into a tight circle, surrounded by a seething horde of grizzly, clawing animated corpses.

The Jiangshi closed in, lurching over those of the number brought down by the guns of the patrol. It took less than a minute for them to be overwhelmed. Han saw comrade after comrade dragged down onto the dirt path and mercilessly set upon. Screams filled the air. The sharp tang of blood filled his nostrils.

He managed somehow to find himself accidentally clear of the vicious, snarling throng. Rifle outstretched, he took a step back. Then another. His comrades were being mercilessly devoured alive. They were beyond help. He didn't dare fire into the clawing mass of Jiangshi for fear of drawing their attention.

He was about to turn and run when the hunched old women saw him. Her bulbous eyes popped wide. She gave a gap-toothed growl, then tossed her head back and howled as she lopsidedly galloped toward him on ankles that seemed to be jumbles of broken bones inside the blue, leathery skin of her legs.

Han raised his rifle, aiming not for her head, but for her distended watermelon belly. He screamed when suddenly the flesh of her belly ripped open and a hideous eyeless, serpentine thing emerged, dripping gore, wide jaw baring rows of needle-sharp teeth, stretching bloodily out of her toward him.

Han pulled his trigger.

The bullet penetrated her rotten abdomen and she exploded. The blast knocked him from his feet and tumbled him backwards along the path. The sound of it sent a high-pitched whistle keening through his ears. White stars circled in front of his eyes. Gore rained down on him. The air was filled with the foul stench of rot. Bits of the worm and the old woman who'd carried it were stuck to his face.

When he looked the force of the blast had scattered the Jiangshi like bowling pins, but they were slowly rising to their feet, turned crimson by the blood and guts of Han's comrades, snarling, and spitting foul foam.

Han needed no further incentive. He turned and fled.

***

Han was one of the very few who had survived such a close encounter with the Jiangshi and as such he constantly found himself drawn to them. He seemed helplessly cursed to have to relive those fateful moments in that remote village. To ponder how his fate and that of Jiangshi had become intrinsically interwoven.

Once the Commissar had finished relaying the day's thought and the assembly was disbanded, he walked closer to the cages and watched the Jiangshi packed inside them. With their swollen bellies, bugged out eyes and marbled flesh they almost looked like exaggerated characters from some Xingtou opera.

But they were unstable and dangerous. Their innards were so full of toxic bile and noxious gases that they could easily explode, as Han had discovered that day. The keepers kept them away from sharp edges. One accidental tear of the flesh and the parasitical worms inside them could slither free and sink their teeth into anyone standing too close. The bars of the cages were wrapped in rags. A spontaneous eruption could set off a chain reaction and destroy an entire cage.

Han had seen this happen.

The Generals were incensed whenever assets were wasted like that.

The first deployment of Jiangshi as weapons of the revolutionary war had been as explosive devices. Half a dozen or so would be sent into Kuomintang encampments disguised as a rag-tag groups of civilian refugees. As soon as they were close enough to extract maximum damage, they would be ignited by sniper bullets.

It filled Han with pride that they had named this technique after his accidental discovery of their potential. *Han Jiguang incendiaries* were far less common than they had been during China's civil war, but they were still, on occasions, utilised for tactical reasons. More likely, however, now the IPLA had acquired an air force, to be dropped out of aircraft hangars in blanket bombardments designed to weaken the infrastructure of urban targets.

As a consequence of coming to the attention of the central committee on that fateful day Han had grown in status. He had seized the opportunities presented to him with a passion. Progressing incrementally upwards in the ranks through selfless acts of working-class heroism, he had acquired chest full of medals.

Before he became a fully-fledged revolutionary, he had transformed himself from chain smoking piano player in a Peking jazz club frequented by decadent westerners to a street fighting firebrand. Now he moved from lowly foot soldier, wading through mud and relentless rain, to section leader, barking at his cohorts, pushing them to the limits of endurance. Finally, he had acquired the honourable status of Political Cadre. His rank entitled him to ride in a wooden cart, hauled by a belligerently bad-tempered mule.

Sometimes he wished the old gang from the jazz clubs could see him now. The saxophonists and horn players, the string plucking double bass men, the drummers and torch singers. They had mocked him when he began attending meetings of the CCP. But where were they now? No doubt they had fled to Formosa with Chiang Kai-shek and his lackeys, only to witness the entire island deliberately overrun with flesh eating Jiangshi.

He wished he'd had the change to re-educate them and change their destiny. Han's primary task was the political education of new conscripts. Despite the impending hostilities, today was to be no exception. His current pupils were an undisciplined bunch of initiates, including Algerian fishermen, Moroccan salt miners and half a dozen fiery washer women. He could see the butchers setting out their tables and laying out the cold corpses of executed prisoners ready for limbs to be sawn off and tossed into the cages by the keepers. Feeding time was not something Han was ever keen on witnessing. He nodded his head, as he always did, as a thank you for the innumerate doors the Jiangshi had opened for him, then turned swiftly on his heels and went to fetch his cart.

With the stubborn mule yawing and trying to pull off in random directions, he led his class to a small, grove of palm trees away from the main encampment. Once the mule was tethered and gnawing on a clump of scraggy yellow grass, Han climbed up onto the cart and addressed the thirty-five pupils sitting in their identical uniforms beneath the long shades of the date palms.

The sun was rising higher now. He could feel the heat slowly baking the back of his neck. He began, as he began each lesson, with a *thought* from the Chairman that he believed to be irrefutable in its insight. "Communists must grasp the truth. The Jiangshi are the masses in their purest form. They are the essence of the masses. They are motivated by a unified purpose and move as a single entity. To emulate them must be the aspiration of every revolutionary fighter."

His personal interpreter translated the words into Arabic.

The pupils found this to be quite amusing, looking at each other, shrugging with fake befuddlement, making slack jawed Jiangshi faces, bugging out their eyes, laughing as they nudged each other in the ribs. Han ignored this. He was a patient teacher. These men and women had accepted conscription because it guaranteed them three meals a day, boots on their feet and a uniform to clothe their backs.

They were not yet true revolutionaries. Nor were they fully acclimatised to the political correctness of revolutionary thought. But it would come. In time they would embrace their class consciousness. Some may even go on to become Cadres themselves.

Today's lesson was on Marxist theology.

"Money," began Han, quoting directly from Das Kapital, "is a commodity, an external object, capable of becoming the private property of an individual."

A slender arm shot up. When Han looked, he wasn't surprised to see who it was. Her name was Fatima. Before the liberation she'd been a seamstress who'd earned a living mending clothes for wealthy Spanish colonists. She was smart and quick witted, always launching questions or making challenges.

Han felt insulted and annoyed by her intervention. Interrupting before he could really get into the swing of his lecture was highly disrespectful. The heat was beginning to agitate the bullet fragment still lodged in the badly healed wound inflicted on him during the fall of Cairo. This was adding to his irritation. Sweat was beading on his forehead. A fruit fly went buzzing noisily past his ear, adding to the discomfort.

There were punishments he could mete out for such insubordination. Have her bitten by a Jiangshi and watch her slowly turn. Hand her over as fodder to the keepers and let them toss her, still alive, into a cage. He had the authority. He could make an example of this upstart, drum some fear into the others into the bargain. But that wasn't the way.

84

There was a saying amongst the Cadres. *Punish one of the uninitiated, turn the others against you. Punish of the initiated, increase the loyalty of your cabal.*

Han drew a deep breath and forced himself to be calm. He nodded his head.

Fatima asked her question.

"What did she say?" Han asked the interpreter.

"She said *what the hell does that mean?*" came the apologetic reply.

At first Han had harboured suspicions that she was continually risking such reckless questions because she might be a counter insurgent infiltrator, tasked with disrupting his lessons. Her commanding officer, however, had given her a glowing report. She was an excellent aim with a rifle and had executed her duties proficiently in a fire fight with a regiment of the French Foreign Legion fleeing the horde of Jiangshi that had been released into their garrison.

Han's latest thought was that she might be a spy of a different sort. Rumours were rife that the Central Committee of the CCP often sent agents to assess the proficiency of Political Cadres. Might this Fatima already outrank him? Might she be clandestinely testing his ability to convey the necessary political correctness? He would hate to think of himself demoted once more to lowly foot soldier.

He tried to explain in simple terms, adopting a cautiously folksy tone that he hoped would not sound too patronizing. He looked at Fatima, addressing her directly. Beneath her peaked cap her long black hair hung in a thick braid over her left shoulder. Her complexion was as dark as molasses. There was mischief in her almond shaped eyes. As he spoke, she pouted at him. He stammered, a little unsettled by this turn of events. The tease of a smile curved at the edges of her lips. The long lashes of her eyelids fluttered.

She's flirting, thought Han. *That's what all these questions are about. She's flirting with me. I hadn't noticed till now.*

This was new. Han had never had the attentions of a woman before. Never had the time. In his younger days he was too fixated on the notion that he would one day travel to America and play piano in a Broadway show to pay much attention to the dancing girls in the clubs. Once he joined the CCP he became too devoted to the cause to entertain such distractions.

He began to blush. The sun felt suddenly much warmer. He could feel embarrassing patches of sweat forming under the armpits of his tunic. The fruit fly buzzed at his ear once more.

Fatima spoke again.

"She says, *thank you,*" relayed the interpreter. "Matters are much clearer in her mind now."

Han gave her a courteous nod of his head. She smiled. Her teeth were gleamingly white and evenly spaced. Han felt an odd flutter in his belly and a little pulsing tattoo thumping in his wrists. He wondered if suggesting some personal tuition might expose an ulterior motive.

Setting the notion aside he cleared his throat and resumed the lecture.

***

When he was first called for, Han thought he was going to be severely reprimanded, punished even, for deserting his comrades. True revolutionaries were expected to die for the cause, not abandon their duty in order to save their own skins. But when he entered the tent and found that it was Zhou Enlai, Chief Political Commissar, seated there, illuminated by the flickering oil lamp, he feared far worse might befall him.

Had his cowardice caused them to dig deep into his past? Had they spoken to those he'd grown up with on the backstreets of Peking? *Oh, Han,* they'd have said. *He was always boasting about how his father was going to come and fetch him and take him on a big ship to America where he would live in the lap of luxury.*

Or had they tracked down some of his former fellow musicians from the jazz clubs? Those who had managed to survive the fall of Formosa? Had they recounted how he used to save as much of his earnings as possible in order to buy a passage across the ocean to his paternal homeland? How his avowed intention was to play piano for the orchestra of a Broadway musical and, in doing so, come to the attention of his estranged father.

Either way he may well have been identified as someone with a propensity for incorrect thought. And that incorrect thought may well now be interpreted as the root cause of his insubordination and dereliction of duty back at the village.

Han's mind began to race, rapidly constructing his defence. He was a true revolutionary these days. He had thrown off his childish notions and embraced class consciousness. He now longer viewed the morally bankrupt United States as the land of milk and honey. No longer harboured any desire whatsoever to find his biological father. Was far more likely to be found playing *The International* for his comrades on a piano than some decadent ragtime tune.

Zhou Enlai waved his hand. Han obediently perched himself on the hard wooden stool that had been set out for him. He could feel a trickle of sweat rolling slowly down his spine. His hands trembled in his lap. He kept his head slightly bowed. He noticed that there was a bell jar sat on the table to Enlai's left. And, in it, a coiled parasitical worm suspended in formaldehyde.

"Tell me about the theory you have been positing, Comrade Han," said Zhou Enlai.

Surprised and slightly wrong footed by the question Han cleared his throat and repeated what he had speculated about with so many others since he staggered back into the camp.

"There was a dog. I believe that the dog bit its master and a worm crept into him. The master bit his wife. The wife bit her child. The child bit her friend. That's how it started. That's why it spread. The worms were passed from one to the next."

"Interesting," said Zhou Enlai. "I wonder, what do you think bit the dog?"

"The dog?" asked Han, still trembling.

"How did the dog become infected?" said the Chief Commissar.

This was something Han had not considered.

"Perhaps the dog went to the forest?" he said. "Perhaps there it encountered a fox or some other creature that was already infected by a worm. Perhaps it was bitten then?"

"Perhaps it was the man who went to the forest," said Zhou Enlai. "Perhaps the man was first bitten. Perhaps it was the man who then bit his dog."

Something else Han had not considered.

Zhou Enlai leaned forward and smiled. "No need to look so anxious, comrade. You have been summoned here in order that I make you aware that you will be decorated with a medal for your heroic deeds."

"Heroic deeds?' Han felt a slight shift in the nature of his tremble.

"For bravery in the face of great adversity," said Zhou Enlai. "And for the vital importance of wonderful discovery you made."

"About the dog?" asked Han.

Zhou Enlai nodded at the bell jar. "About the worm. About how we may use this to our advantage. How we might weaponise the 'so called' Jiangshi. And how this may alter the fortunes of the revolution."

And thus, Han was anointed by the Chief Political Commissar himself.

And thus, his fortunes changed.

***

89

The British bombardment commenced at dusk. Big Howitzers firing shells from the fortified dock on Gibraltar, scattering the little boats that had been dispatched out into the swell to taunt the imperialist. Gunships moving cautiously into range, their captains clearly on edge because of the rumours central intelligence in Peking had spread about the acquisition of enemy submarines.

Preparations had been made. The twelve battalions had dispersed and moved underground like a vast termite army. For days they had been digging and fortifying tunnels. A maze-like labyrinth now connected the buildings and basements of the former Spanish protectorate. Decoys had been set. Mannequin soldiers gathered around fires in abandoned encampments. Wooden rifles and mortars on gritty lips of fake defensive trenches. Balsawood trucks guarding empty munitions dumps.

In one section of the tunnels the tow trucks had dragged their trains of cages and set them in a long column. Between the juddering explosions Han could hear the keening and growling of the agitated Jiangshi. They were building up a bloodlust that would be unstoppable once they were released onto Gibraltar's jagged shoreline.

Let the British squander their artillery chasing fool's gold, thought Han. *Let them exhaust themselves in this nocturnal folly. Let them turn back for Gibraltar, patting themselves on the back at what they believed to be a successful mission. They will face the blood thirsty reality of the Jiangshi onslaught soon enough.*

As befitting a Cadre, Han had been allocated a curtained section of a fortified basement in which to sleep on his bedroll. The ground juddered and the walls shuddered from overhead explosions. Han checked his face in the cracked fragment of a mirror he carried in his pack. Eyes too round and odd in their blueness. Pencil thin moustache set above his top lip, grown when he had been promoted to Cadre in an effort to give himself an air of authority.

With his part western heritage was he handsome, or ugly, or just plain? He didn't know. It wasn't a question that had ever occurred to him before. He guessed, as the saying went, all of that was in the eye of the beholder. With a shrug he put the mirror away, sent for his interpreter and asked him to fetch Fatima.

She was still dressed in her uniform, but the braiding had been unravelled and her lush black hair was cascading over her shoulders. Her head was slightly bowed, as if she didn't dare to look him in the eye. When he saw her Han felt his breath tremble inside him.

She turned to the interpreter and whispered something.

"She wants to know if you are going to reprimand her for asking so many questions," said the interpreter.

Han shook his head. "Tell her she has an enquiring mind, which is a good thing. But she should save her questions until the end of the lecture, instead of always interrupting."

The interpreter translated.

Fatima lifted her chin and nodded solemnly to show she understood. Their eyes met again and Han felt his heart do a somersault. His pulse quickened. He felt the dull throb of it in his old bullet wound. She whispered to the interpreter.

"She wants to know if that was the reprimand," he said. "Or if there is something else you wish to discuss."

Brazen to a fault, thought Han, finding the wherewithal not to chuckle out loud.

A shell hit nearby. Dust fell on the three of them. The Jiangshi roared in the tunnels, as if convinced that bombardment would release them from their cages and permit the blood-fuelled rampage they desired. Fatima almost lost her balance but managed to grab the interpreter's elbow to steady herself. She straightened up and cast a cheeky grin in Han's direction. He blushed and smiled back at her.

"Tell her..." he said to the interpreter. Suddenly he felt embarrassed. Somewhat sweaty and fidgety. Unsure if he had the courage to relay what he wished to say. He loosened the collar on his tunic and swallowed down the dry lump that came to his throat.

"What is it you want me to tell her?" asked the interpreter.

Han gave a little cough. "Tell her I like her," he said.

The interpreter scratched at the whiskers on his bristly chin and cocked his head.

"Are you sure you want me to tell her that?"

Had nodded.

The interpreter relayed what he'd said.

92

Fatima looked at him, dark eyebrows raised over dark eyes.

"She says she likes you too," said the interpreter once she'd replied.

Han didn't know what to say now. A tremble vibrated through him.

Fatima whispered something to the interpreter.

"She says you are both like children in the playground. Passing messages between a mutual friend."

The three of them laughed.

Fatima said something else.

"She says that if you order it, she will sleep with you tonight," the interpreter relayed.

Han felt mortified.

"No, no, no," he insisted. "I would never pull rank and order such a thing."

Another shell hit nearby. The Jiangshi roared in dreadful unison. Fatima fell sideways from the impact. The interpreter grabbed her before she hit the wall. "Both of you go back to your stations," ordered Han. "Tell her we will speak again tomorrow evening."

Fatima smiled at him again when the words were passed on.

Han felt a sense of lightness and elation beyond anything he'd ever experienced before.

***

Sleep evaded Han. It wasn't just the shelling. It was Fatima. Whenever he closed his eyes, he saw her face, lips pouting, eyes teasing him. Whenever he

93

tried to redirect his thoughts to question of class consciousness and class struggle, they somehow redirected themselves back to Fatima. He wondered if he should speak to the Commissar in the morning. Confess to this infatuation before he became wholly distracted.

No, he thought. *That would be interpreted as a sign of weakness. An indication that his political commitment was not as solid as it might be.*

He told himself not to worry so much. Relationships were permitted so long as they did not interfere with the core objectives of the cause. There was a balance to be achieved. He could do this. He could carry out his duties as a Cadre with the due diligence required and still engage in a courtship with Fatima. He just had to discipline and focus himself.

But sleep continued to evade him. When the bombardment finally ceased, he rose from his bunk and crept slowly in amongst the cages lined up in the tunnels. The Jiangshi had fallen silent. They stood side by side, still as statues, bulging eyes staring into the distance, feet buried in the filthy straw which lined the floors of the cages. Han covered his face with a scarf against the rotting stench of them.

It had been posited that this trancelike state was their equivalent of sleep. Han imagined that this was how the Jiangshi had been standing in mist that fateful first day amongst the rice paddies. Their sleep, though was light, easily disturbed. It only took one of them to become aroused for the whole horde to transform into a seething, agitated mass, growling and foaming, bumping pot bellies as they turned that way and this.

Therefore, emulating their stillness and silence was of the utmost importance. Han spread his legs slightly to maintain balance and measured his breath. It was like a meditation. He often came here in the mornings. To settle his mind. To readjust his equilibrium. To attune himself to the pure essence of the masses. For Han this was a far more effective way of centring himself that the Tai Chi exercises so many of his comrades espoused.

When the Jiangshi were quiet and still like this there was an uncanny peace to be found amongst them. Measuring his breath Han observed how their blue flesh gleamed from the oily excretions that oozed from their pores. How their rotted eyelids drooped but did not entirely close over the impossible bulge of their eyeballs. How stretched and smooth the skin was over their blown bellies, jagged veins forking over the curve. How their bellies occasionally twitched to the shifting and resettling of the things that lived within them.

Inside, their organs were liquefied. Whatever they devoured fell into this well of acidity where it was digested through slow corrosion. The Jiangshi were walking methane repositories. This was what made them so volatile.

Post-mortem vivisection had revealed that each Jiangshi hosted a single coiled parasitical worm, nestled in their bellies. As Han had witnessed these creatures were eyeless and blind. Barbs on their spiny albino backs kept them attached to the stomach lining. Wide jaws filled with double rows

95

of serrated teeth relentlessly fed on the rancid soup that sloshed around them.

The theory ran that chemicals within their excreta infected the brains of their hosts and were what transformed colonised humans into flesh eating monsters whose only purpose was to satisfy the voracious appetites of these carnivorous interlopers. The bile ejaculated from their reproductive organs contained the eggs that infected the blood stream. You did not die if you were bitten by a Jiangshi. You underwent a metamorphosis. The change was said to be agonising. It could take hours, sometimes days, for a freshly hatched worm to grow sufficiently to fully seize control and make its lair in your belly.

This was what was known so far. It was said an entire laboratory complex had been constructed on the outskirts of Peking devoted to research and study of the parasites. But no one had yet established what had first bitten the farmer and his dog, or, indeed, which of them had been bitten first.

***

The landscape was pock marked with shell craters. Acrid smoke wafted in the air but the sun was up and the silk banners depicting the image of Chairman Mao were already erected and fluttering in the breeze blowing in from the sea.

Over on the Rock of Gibraltar the enemy generals no doubt slept soundly in their beds, believing they'd left a good night's work behind them. They were to be permitted two more such nights of delusion before the air raids commenced and the gun boats were brought from their secret coves to transport the Jiangshi across the straights.

The Commissar climbed up onto her munitions box and held the loud hailer to her mouth to relay the daily thought. "Without the necessary restraint of the CCP and its revolutionary vanguard the Jiangshi infection would rapidly develop into an unstoppable pandemic," she recited. "The foundations of civilisation would crumble and society would collapse. But our class enemies amongst the capitalists and imperialists are both wily and cunning. They would invest all of their considerable resources into contingencies. Thus, would be prepared to rise like a Phoenix from the ashes to establish a feudal order far worse than the system of exploitation fired by industrialisation.

It is therefore the duty of every communist to do all that is humanly possible to utilise the Jiangshi in the sole advancement of the revolutionary objectives of the proletariat. And, in doing so, change the course of history forever."

The battalions cheered as she repeated the thought in various languages. Han felt the pride swell within him once more. He was full of admiration for the runners who had managed to memorise every word in order to relay the thought from one section of the Great March to another.

The battalions began to disperse in order to carry out their duties for the day. Han considered the structure of his lecture. Today's subject was *What Is to Be Done?* A treatise by Vladimir Lenin. Han knew it by heart. He very much hoped that now their mutual attraction had been openly stated Fatima would see fit not to continually interrupt him.

He wasn't sure though that his mule could cope with two more nights in an underground stable. It was becoming increasingly delinquent and irritable. It pulled the cart past the Jiangshi cages making it brayed and kicked its heels.

In spite of the subterranean defences, the night had not been without casualties. Two dozen men and women had been crushed to death in a tunnel collapse. Their mangled bodies had been set out in an unkempt pile. The butchers were already at work at their tables. The keepers were filling buckets with the pink slop of gutted innards. Sensing blood in the air, the Jiangshi were severely agitated.

They truly are the essence of the masses, thought Han, *unified by a single thought and purpose.* He pushed on to the grove of date palms where his cohorts were already seated in their shade, Fatima amongst them. Not wishing to be distracted he avoided looking directly at her as he tethered the mule and climbed up onto the cart.

Han cleared his throat and called the class to order. Chattering stopped and heads turned toward him. They were becoming more obedient and attentive. That was good sign. Fatima caught his eye, smiled and nodded her head as if offering encouragement. Feeling buoyed, he smiled back.

By way of introduction, he began by emphasizing the importance of the Bolshevik revolution. The mule seemed intent on sabotaging him. Its constant yawning was disturbing the flow of the lecture and drowning out his voice. If it pulled out the wooden stake to which it was tethered it would surely gallop away. Then what would he do?

There was another distraction too. A much deeper one. Fatima had now seated herself under the date palm closest to him. Her hair was braided again and hanging demurely over her left shoulder. Every time he caught a glimpse of her, she'd pout and flutter her eyelashes. It caused him to stammer and lose his train of thought.

He wondered if she was a virgin like he was. He hoped so. He had no experience whatsoever of women. No clue as to what might be expected of him. If she was as inexperienced as him, then the two of them could go on a voyage of discovery. Wouldn't that be something?

A shout went up, interrupting his thoughts. From the sky there came the low drone of an engine. When Han looked up a single aircraft was arcing inland from the coast. Everyone fell to the ground, hands over their heads. Han scrambled under the cart, dragging his interpreter with him. The mule panicked, kicking its heels and pulling at its tether.

Han could see Fatima, crouched low behind the trunk of the palm. Their eyes met. He felt another delicious tremble run through him. He wondered if he should crawl to her. Protect her with his body. Wasn't that the chivalrous thing to do in such situations?

He was about to launch himself into action when he saw that what was falling out of sky was not a rain of bullets but hundreds and hundreds of leaflets, fluttering like a swarm of inky moths. One landed close to the wheel of the cart. The interpreter grabbed it.

"It's in Spanish," he said.

"Can you read Spanish?" asked Han.

The interpreter nodded. "Yes, yes."

"Then read, damn you," snapped Han. "Tell me what it says."

The interpreter paraphrased.

"Franco has been deposed. His execution is imminent. Entire regiments of the Spanish Nationalist army are defecting to the Republican cause. Madrid is in the hands of the Republicans once more. The Republican command has pledged allegiance to the International Peoples Liberation Army. A branch of the Great March, resplendent with Jiangshi cages, has entered Spain at Andorra. The British are evacuating."

So, Franco had capitulated rather than face a Jiangshi onslaught.

The British were surrounded now. No wonder they were fleeing.

"Proclaim this joyous news," said Han, pointing to his pupils, still cowering amongst the palms. "Another dictator toppled. Gone the way of those fascist upstarts Mussolini and Hitler."

Han crawled out, reached up into his cart and fetched his binoculars from their leather casing. He heard the cheering as the interpreter explained what had happened. When Han placed the lenses to his eyes, he could see the British ships were already leaving. In the face of the pincer movement against them, they were abandoning their colony.

100

Han trained his binoculars on the pale and jagged Rock of Gibraltar. He had heard it was inhabited by wild monkeys. Once they'd made the crossing, he would get his interpreter to ask Fatima to stroll up there with him. As the moon rose over the Mediterranean, he would take her hands in his. If she would permit it, he would kiss her.

Afterwards he would explain to the Commissar that they were together. Fatima would be allowed to ride at his side in the cart. They would engage in endless political discourse. In Arabic or Mandarin, whichever turned out to be easiest for the other. They would sleep in a lover's embrace on a straw mattress at the back of the cart.

When the Jiangshi swarmed their cities and Great Britain finally fell and the Armada eventually assembled to transport the Great March across the mighty Atlantic, they would board their designated ship hand in hand, the inspiring *thoughts* of the Chairman lighting revolutionary fires in their bellies.

And, when, the Jiangshi overran the cradle of capitalism and proletarian classes of the USA and Canada rose against their oppressors, they would be there with them, taking over the means of production, helping establish urban soviets. Their victory was inevitable. Silk banners would flutter on Broadway and Wall Street. Mao's words would echo over Times Square.

Han would be exactly where he once dreamed of being. Only the reality would be vastly different to that naïve, youthful dream. A piano would be requisitioned from one of the theatres. He'd play

101

The International and the massed battalions would sing to the high heavens in glorious revolutionary fervour.

Word had it that already vast Solidarity Marches were assembling in Panama and Honduras. Insurgent peasants and tenant farmers in Mexico and the Caribbean were seizing plantations from land-owning oligarchs. Far north the gargantuan unified arm of the Great March, which included Bolshevik and Red Army soldiers, was assembling at the Baring Straight, ready to cross over to Alaska. It was said that the traitor Stalin was himself in one of the Jiangshi cages, foam and gore dripping from his infamous moustache.

Glorious days lay ahead of them. Their children would be born into a world where the masses had shaken off the chains of their oppression. Where all men and women were truly equal and worked in communal unity to perpetuate the glorious cause of the global revolution. By then the Jiangshi would have served their purpose and the stated plan to humanely slaughter them in vast industrial complexes would have been diligently executed.

Han was so enthralled by the idealistic whimsy of this fantasy that he didn't hear Fatima creeping up behind him. The blade of her bayonet plunged deep into his back. He turned and fell, saw her laugh, and curse him in Arabic before a bullet to the head took her out.

She was a proficient assassin. He was losing copious amounts of blood. As he lay in paralysis in the dirt the interpreter pressed his calloused hand down hard on the wound, desperately trying to staunch the flow. But Han knew it was too late. He became seized by the wave of dizziness that was dragging him down into the deep, inevitable pit of death.

His only solace was the fact that his original suspicions about Fatima were confirmed. Had he only been true to his instincts! Not distracted by the childish nonsense of romance. Nevertheless, news of his death would serve a practical purpose. Fatima's duplicity would make Political Cadres more alert to the risk of infiltration by counter insurgents. The running dogs of imperialism would thus be efficiently brought to heel.

Han would no doubt receive a posthumous medal. They would erect a statue with a brass plaque in his honour at this lonely spot amongst the date palms. Many such statues stood along the length and breadth Great March. As the March progressed from victory to victory the IPLA had developed an appetite for martyrs as voracious as that of the Jiangshi parasites.

He could see Fatima only a foot or so away from him. Skull split by the bullet. Blood pooling around her head. Black flies descending like mourners. She would be drawn and quartered for Jiangshi fodder. He gazed into her glassy, dead eyes.

It might have been nice though, he pondered. *To have loved, and to have been loved.*

Now there was a thought to go out on.

In the distance he saw the approach of one of the keepers. She was dragging a naked male Jiangshi behind her, manacled and muzzled, waddling bow legged beneath its bloated belly. If they were going to have it bite him and pass a worm into him before he expired, they'd better hurry.

Waste not want not, as the saying went. By sunset he would be caged, growling and foaming at the mouth, belly beginning to swell as the voracious parasite grew inside him and fired his appetite. Finally, he would become a fully-fledged member of the masses. Perhaps Fatima would provide his first taste of human flesh.

The keeper removed the muzzles and pressed the head of her Jiangshi to his neck. Its teeth bit deep into the flesh and tore away a bloody chunk of muscle tissue. Han screamed from the agony of it. He imagined the eggs now passing from the sour saliva into his blood stream. One of them eventually hatching into a worm.

Would it be different having a parasite direct his thoughts rather than the Chairman? If all went to plan, he would one day walk down Broadway, ahead of the Great March. Or, at the very least, shuffle under the crown of a stretched belly, observing the neon lights through bulging eyes, setting on those who fled the Jiangshi advance, tearing flesh from bone. To the very end making his contribution to the advancement of the revolution.

One thing was certain though.

He would never again play piano.

Yin Yang (SJ Townend)

I wake at midnight with a gasp of pain. Father said I was born with pain inside me; it will always be a part of who I am. I wonder—is it the same pain I saw in his dead eyes before I closed them for the final time? And if it is, did his hurt pour into me or mine into him?

The thing with dagger-blade teeth which imprison an even sharper tongue has been with me ever since I found Father. Lop ears roll down its sides and drag along the floor. It creeps, it pours; it dresses in shadows. Its hearing is impeccable. I cry in silence each evening when it's near because if a single, grey tear splashes on my beige pillowcase, it'll pounce and pin me down and slap me into and through dreadful slumber. From dawn the following day, I'll be seven shades tired and it'll loosely follow me, haunting my heart, forcing me to see life through its black-blood-stained lens. I'll spend the morning trying to shake it off. I'll douse it with cheap whisky to block out its cruel whispers, and then fall into an abyss of daymare-filled, restless sleep.

Only I can see it, but we all sense its presence. My partner says he knows it's here by my aura, the way I don't wear my hair and the fact I refuse to leave the house. Through these dark days he'll take over childcare, the chores. *Mummy's having a moment.* And through these periods, he'll sleep in the box room.

"No Sam, not tonight," my husband will say to our boy while searching for diplomatic phrasing, my actions having made a lighthouse of me. "Mummy needs the bed to herself. If you wake and can't resettle, come hop in with me."

I gasp for air again and clutch my sore chest. Bed sheets sodden with dank sweat swim stale beneath me, but at least my bed is my own again and now, minutes past midnight, I once more feel alive.

It's gone.

Before I woke, in the last moments of my nightmare, I swear I heard it jump down from my chest and scurry off.

My ribcage, now freed to breathe deeply, feels bruised. The veil of darkness and tiredness, the sadness that dripped from me, that flooded our family for days, weeks, a month, has lifted. My lungs ache because I can inhale again without resistance.

***

I've done little but sleep and cry since I found and buried Father. But this isn't grief, not wholly— Father and I weren't close. At all. His death may've triggered this down phase, who knows, but this cyclic curse has movements no scientist or prophet can predict.

Now, my head feels clear. I rub sleep from my eyes. The body odour stench I've allowed to manifest suddenly disgusts me. It's the middle of the night, witching hour and I'm fully awake. I stretch out the pain which I can now rename 'relief'.

***

12.13am. In the quiet of the night, I shed my clothing and climb in the shower. Here, I sing to myself—loudly enough to entertain a small money spider (now the only thing watching me), quietly enough not to wake my family. Once dry, I cross the landing and take in the night-time beauty of my two favourite sleeping souls. The pair are curled up together, a mesh of dark curls, freckles and Snoopy duvet. Glorious. So still, it is if they appear dead. The thought of ever losing them sends a shudder down my spine. I will surely go first. At times, when I am down, I feel already like a ghost drifting amongst them. But not now, now I feel electrified, fully charged, as if Death will never come to greet me.

In my kitchen, I pour tea and load up my online shopping basket with doorstep-delivered art supplies: white spirit, badger-hair brushes, acrylics and oils. I don't know how long this uptime stint will last—no-one knows—but now, in this moment, lightning is bolting through my vessels where blood ran blue-cold before and with it flows an overpowering urge: buy, sing, create, dance, move. Twelve thirty am. Time to paint.

Productivity comes in bursts and fits and I've not lifted a brush for weeks. I sink my tea and note I've several hours 'til sunrise, so, eager as wildfire, I head out to our garage-cum-art studio. The swinging lamp stutters on and with it comes the

107

radio. I yank off the hessian sacks, dusters and rags which I tossed over my paintings the moment the darkness crept over me last time and stand—hands on hips—and stare.

With biased eyes, it's nigh impossible to see the good and bad within each piece, the black and the white, but I do see the quality in what I do. I see why people say I've talent, why my work sells, yet I still struggle to like any of my paintings. And that is why they remain here, strung up in the garage, a wall of faces. Forty-three portraits to be precise.

At first I painted family—living and long gone— from photos and memory and once I'd drawn every blood connection, I drew the sparse friends I've clung onto over the years. Then, I started to paint, quite obsessively, everyone I came into contact with: Myra who runs the village shop, our postman, the checkout girl who doesn't do small talk whom I always make a beeline for if she's free, random parents at the school gate whom I interact with for just long enough to capture the essence and symmetry of their faces. Everyone I ever meet.

I've a style, it's fair to say. Every face is true to form, vivid. Each is a diverse celebration of the individual; however, each portrait shares one common flaw for which I forever beat myself up. But it seems to be the reason galleries book me, the feature critics always praise: the eye contact—or rather, lack of—that each image portrays. Each face carries eyes which do anything but follow you round the room.

**

108

I mount a canvas on my easel, squirt out primer on my palette and mull, but I've no idea who to paint— I haven't left the house in six days so I decide once more to try to capture *it* on canvas, the thing that haunts me. But when it's not with me—and I feel it's far, far away right now—when it's not burning its snout against mine and its claws of smoke and hate aren't anchored to my breast, I've no idea what it looks like. So now, in the midst of the night, with surplus energy than anyone else could ever care for, I draw a blank.

***

I put my brush down. With a journey to make in the morning, I figure I'll find a new project then. I twist up the volume dial, close my eyes and dance and when I get bored, I play with hoarded garage junk: clothing, books, box-fresh devices to spiralize vegetables, endless tat I've ordered in a frenzy of mind. Rarely bin anything, even packaging and when I'm not being sat upon and I'm jaunting on a high, if I'm not painting, or singing, or dancing, or online shopping, I'm organising. When the hellish cloud that looms is not around, I always find something that needs to be done.

***

Must've dozed off around five. My partner wakes me with decaf coffee and a smile.

109

"Get much done, love?" he asks. I feel incandescent in his love. Never reprimands, never judges, no matter how far along either end of the see-saw I'm lost. The only aspect of me we've ever come to verbal blows over is medication: makes me sleepy, gain a few pounds. However, he's quite polar on the matter. But prescriptions make a piano of only white keys of me; I become unable to play the sad songs, and sometimes, we need the sad songs, for balance.

"No painting, no," I say and take the mug and return the smile. "But I packed down all the delivery boxes. And date-ordered all the National Geographics." I point to a mountainous stack of cardboard and a large crate.

"Lovely. I'm sure that'll be helpful, you know, next time we need to rapidly find an article about—" his eyes flit to the box." —'*Why Jamaican Reggae and Finnish Saunas have UNESCO status*'." I punch him playfully in the belly.

"We've three hundred and thirty-one editions, " I say and slurp the bitter liquid.

He reaches out his hand, places it on top of mine which is digging into my breastbone. He holds it still, tight, quietens my busy hand. I've been scratching at my birthmark unaware. I fiddle with my port wine stain when manic.

"You okay to have Sam today? I need to go in," he says. It's the school holidays. A pang of guilt hits. He's taken the last few days off work to care for our son whilst I've been having 'downtime'.

"Yes. Busy day ahead, actually. Bit of an adventure on the cards," I say and march him back into the

110

house. "I'm going to pick up the tin. Sam can play driver's mate."

"If you're sure."

And I've never been surer.

***

My father dealt with most of his belongings himself before he got really ill. But after he died, a hospice nurse called me. He'd given her a tin to hold onto, to pass onto me. I've not felt up to the drive until today but right now, I'm jonesing to discover— what did he feel was so important for me to have?

I let Sam sit in the front next to me. Says he feels safer here, the front has airbags. (I drive like I talk when I'm out and about: fast. Always. There's never enough time to fit everything in.) I look at all seven years of my son and feel a volcanic eruption of pride and dopamine exploding in my heart. His smile often moves me to tears. Happy tears. Not the tears that come when I can't leave my bedroom and my chest is gripped in a night-vice.

We chat for the duration of the trip, or I chat, Sam nods and smiles. As we pull up in the hospice car park, Sam says he doesn't want to get out, come in, and I understand. The building emits an ode of death with its infrastructure all Rivers Styx and Acheron, so I rush in and out and bring back the tin and ponder, shall I, coalmine canary, peek first, alone?

My father was a dark soul, but I'm convinced he wouldn't leave me anything unsuitable for young eyes. The one time he met Sam, he showered him

111

with warmth. My son received more birthday cards and posted gifts from Father than I ever did. I say, "Let's open it together," and Sam's face lights up. His happiness is the wind beneath my wings and today I'm soaring high.

We drive to a cafe and I treat us both to hot chocolates. Sam touches me on the arm, all wide-eyed, a frame of panic to his face. "You're bleeding, Mum," he says. I reach for a napkin and dab at my chest. Without realising, I've taken off the top layer of my fist-sized birthmark swirl.

Shaped and shaded like a two-tone yin-yang, half of it's crimson, the other side, pale pink. Hermann Rorschach might see two entwined lovers, curled speech marks, or two tadpoles looped together, each with an eye the colour of the other. I see a yin-yang symbol, the melding of two opposites. I was bullied for it at school, but I've come to accept it's just another part of who I am.

"So I am. I'm such a naughty picker." The bleeding eases and leaves small, pinprick balls of red cresting my skin. I reassure: *Mummy is fine*. Sam calms and I let myself become distracted by the waiting staff, the lady behind the counter, patrons. My mind's eye is rampant. It documents and stores every face. I will paint them all later, once Sam's gone to bed.

"Let's open the tin, shall we?" I say. I let him lift off the metal lid. Inside is a slip of paper and an old sepia photograph: a clearing in a wood. Sam, expecting cash, is disappointed. I pull a twenty from my purse and tell him to go and choose a piece of cake, *keep the change.* Sam approaches the counter and grins at the spread of fondant fancies.

112

I turn over the sheet of paper and try to make sense of it. A single word, 'sorry', is scrawled in the centre. Around it are seven names which I read over, again and again. One name is Father's, another, Mother's. She died when I was small. The other five names however, I've no clue. And what is most peculiar? They're all written in a circle, spread around the sheet like numbers on a clock.

***

Before we leave the cafe, I need to make a call. Sam is sticky-fingered, content, so I sneak outside and dial the only lady I can think of who may be able to help me interpret this puzzle.

I pace through all seventeen rings until she answers the phone.

"Yes."

"Hi. Martha? It's me."

Ice follows. We spoke briefly at Father's funeral, made polite exchanges, praised the floral arrangements, but prior to that? We've not spoken in years.

Silence. I know she's still at the end of the line, I can hear the crackle of elderly lungs. Martha is my grandmother. Father's mother.

"It's about Father."

"Gathered so."

"Can I come over?"

"Not today. Frightfully busy."

She's ninety-six, the oldest person I've ever painted. Her face hangs top left in my garage gallery. Her

113

oil-paint, grey-fish-eyes—like those in all my other paintings—stare anywhere but at your own.

"Of course," I say. "Of course." I tell her, quick-fire, about the tin and its contents and just ask outright if she can help before she hangs up. "Any ideas? What does it mean?"

Silence. I can see an outline of Sam through the frosted cafe window. He's getting restless, the sugar's kicking in. I dab at my raw chest and continue to rattle back and forth along the pavement outside the cafe.

"Can't help you, dear." I sense a change in her tone. Less Victorian matriarch, more lost sheep. She's pulled back from the phone mouthpiece.

"Really? Nothing?" I say, patience thinning.

"I expect it's just his way of apologising."

"For what? Is this to do with Mum?"

"Not directly, dear. More to do with you." A long pause ensues. "You, and the way you are. I suggest you read nothing more into it." And with that, she hangs up.

And there's nothing I need more in my life right now than to read more into it.

I place the items back into this Pandora's box from Father, go back in to shimmy Sam out, and cheetah back to the car.

***

We drive to a park so Sam can play and I can dig on the move. Double-time, I stroll around the perimeter with my eyes set firm on my phone screen. My folks were local people so I probe locally: village

114

pub, corner shop, bowling green. I cyber-stalk and click and call multiple names and numbers in search of the five contacts on the circle-shaped list, all the while I draft and redraft possible explanations in my mind.

Father's dead.

Mother's dead.

Three of the other members of the circle also turn out to be dead. This comes as no great surprise—my parents were old when they had me.

Number six is alive. Bingo.

I contact his relatives to learn he has dementia—doesn't remember who they are, let alone the names of my parents when I ask after them.

I've one name left, Margaret Millard. Alive. And now, after sweet-talking the penultimate connection, I also have her address.

Since the stroke of midnight, my mind has been switched to 'on'. Neural messages are surging fast, making a computer processor of my brain. I lean against a tree and close my eyes to rest but all I see is cerebral-fire. I see, feel, breathe, the warm, frenetic buzz of flickering Christmas tree lights mid-July. I can accomplish more in a day when I'm out of the deep end of the lagoon of my sickness than I could in a lifetime of treading water. Or so it feels. There's nothing I can't do right now—except rest.

"Sam," I yell. He looks up from the top of the wooden pirate ship. "We're going."

***

115

Margaret lets us in. Her eyes radiate a kindness. She brings us fruit loaf and tea and directs Sam to a box of toys she keeps for her own grandchildren.

I show Margaret the photo. "That's the clearing half-way up Three-Mile-Hill, before you reach the farm. Haven't been up there for years." She flags up the walking stick propped by the front door then shrugs at her own knees.

Her words flow tardily, or, I'm processing them too quickly.

"Why would he leave me a photo of it? And why's your name part of this circle?" I say and push the slip towards her.

She stalls, offers more tea, travels to the kitchen and back to gather a tub of sugar and a teaspoon.

"Do you really want to know, dear?"

I've both feet in now, in this dang circle. I'm draped over the edge of this precipice, this cryptic death-slide. Whatever truth she's retaining, I won't be leaving until I hear it.

"Of course," I say. She looks over at Sam. He's caught in a fantasy of yellowed, plastic farm animals, a variety of dolls.

"It was a meeting."

"A what?"

"A séance meeting. More of an offering, really. Séances were usually held indoors." Margaret, eyes narrow, head tilted back, appears to be studying the images her memories are creating.

"And these were the people involved?" I ask.

"Yes."

"In the woods?"

116

"Your mother, lovely woman. Struggling to conceive."

I push the biscuit around the edge of my saucer and feel the furrow in my brow deepen.

"A small sacrifice was made. Didn't go so well first time. We had to go back up."

"I'm sorry, what? A sacrifice—?"

"It was dark, of course—these things are always done at night—and as we were stood spread out in our circle, none of us could catch it. Mr. Bream managed to nick it, I think. I could see its fear though. Beetle-black, beady eyes. I remember seeing the glint of its blood on its white fur by the light of the paraffin lamps we'd placed at the five points of the star. But none of us could move fast enough to catch it."

"Catch what?" My voice comes out loud.

Sam looks up. "Mummy?"

"It's alright, love. Won't be long."

"Mummy, your neck."

"Oh dear, your neck's bleeding." Margaret passes me a tissue. I dab at the edge of the tip of the yin I've been subconsciously shredding.

"Catch what?" I say again.

"The rabbit. To evoke new life in your mother, to help ease you into this spiritual plane, Mr. Bream needed to sacrifice something. One-in, one-out, if you like."

"Someone killed a rabbit?"

"He failed first time. Poor little white bugger didn't stand a chance in the woods at night though, stood out like a sore thumb. It was already bleeding heavily as it skittered off into the darkness. Such a

117

lively one. Spirited. We all wanted to carry on, but he said we needed to make the full sacrifice in the centre of the circle. Something needed to die in the centre."

"Fuck." I feel tension creep into my shoulders. The tissue is sodden with red. Margaret proffers a clean one.

"You went back?"

"Yes." She pauses, shifts in her seat. "Sure you want me to continue? You're white as a sheet, duck."

Mother had been desperate to conceive, Father said she was over the moon when she found out she was pregnant. The only time I saw pure love in his eyes was when he spoke of her. I fell pregnant easily with Sam but I can understand the drive, the urge to become a parent. But this? This is ludicrous. Otherworldly. No wonder Father didn't tell me this. Mother died shortly after giving birth to me, and Father, despite raising me solo, grew emotionally distant. His heart hardened.

"Yes. Please. I need to know." I'm welling up. In the well-lit room, a dark shadow pours out from behind Margaret's chair, onto her rug. "Please."

"We returned with a fresh rabbit the following week. A black one. Runtish, sick-looking thing. All bones, no meat. It was the last in the shop, we had no choice. We went ahead anyway, despite the manual specifying 'white'. The candle of time was burning fast for your mother. She was pushing forty."

"What happened to that rabbit?"

118

"Slashed from neck to tail under a strong moon. Gave up more than enough blood to cover your mother's stomach. Your father drank a half-pint, then vomited into the emptiness of the forest behind him."

"Jesus—"

"He wasn't involved, dear. Not in our church."

"—Christ"

"You came along nine months later—one bonny baby for the price of two, scrappy kits. She was overjoyed. Such a shame she passed so soon after."

I feel sick. I collect my scrambled thoughts, thank her for the tea, grab Sam, and leave.

***

Should I drive to the forest, find the spot where this ritual occurred? I just can't. Sam asks over and over: "Why are you crying, Mummy?" But I can't and won't burden him with the filth I've just heard. Every time I look in the rear view mirror to overtake, switch lanes as I shuttle home at breakneck speed, I see the creeping shadow.

It's back. Ribbons of darkness spool from the back seat of my car into the driver's footwell. Tendrils of sadness and doom roll under my chair and weave up and around me. Cruel whispers only I can hear begin again: *You're worthless, nothing.* I feel it in my lap, weighting me down. It plucks at my heart strings with talons of melancholy. Only I can hear the coercive swansong it plays. It's back, and I need to get home and in my room.

I'm a mess when I pull up. My partner eases me out of my clothes, into my pyjamas, and tucks me up in bed.

An hour passes. In the darkness, I hear it panting, twitching, waiting to hurl itself onto me. I'm exhausted but I don't want it to drag me back down its slope. I know it's stronger in the dark, so I reach for and switch on the bedside light and watch it recoil into the corner, with its long, black ears of velvetine fog and a face I can never remember when I'm up and well enough to paint. But now, I see it with clarity. It makes a shaking child of my heart. White, empty eyes glower at me, vacant yet filled with the magnitude and permanence of death. It whisper-shouts: *Séance Girl. Child of Séance.*

I drag myself out of bed. I have to push on through this depth of despair and woe. I hiss at it. In a skirmish, it vanishes beneath the bed. By the dim light of the bedside table, I dress, then check on my husband and child. Fast asleep. On the landing, I cry in silence. It's better Sam doesn't see me like this, safer.

Safer without you.

Safer without me? My son's safer without me?

I stumble down the stairs and head out to the garage.

It's close. Draining me. I must paint it away. I can see it, I can picture it. If I trap it on canvas, it may no longer have power. I'm not thinking straight.

I swirl black and white on a palette and fling and dash until the stretched canvas in front of me is splattered. It's awash with everything but colour: emotion, contrast, bipolarity.

Useless. Terrible.

This piece does not feel like it's helping. I abandon it, pick up a fresh canvas. The last thing I feel like doing as I writhe around at the bottom of this pit is painting, but paint I must.

I churn out image after image of everyone I've seen today. They are poor pieces. My radiant muse isn't present, just this beast of darkness. The people in the nursing home, the waitress, Margaret, Mr Bream, (although we never met), Mother and Father in their prime, the others from the circle. Up and up go more and more bad portraits, and of course, none of them are looking at me. I've never managed to master eyes.

I'm being torn in two directions. Siamese twin babies, Yin and Yang, connected at the hip, are each trying to crawl free.

No-one should exist with two spirits in one skin.

Almost every ounce of oxygen is sucked from my blood, squeezed from my orifices as it presses up against me. I recline on the cold, concrete floor and let it take its place on my tired chest.

Liberate me.

On my ribcage, this thing, dark as funeral pyre smoke, white devil eyes, stares directly into my soul, my two, trapped souls.

Séance child. Should not be here.

And I realise, it is right. This is why I lead this life of pain. Why I swing pendulous, an unstable chandelier, from one peak to the next, stopping only to sit in the trough of the nether whilst my brain fails.

Should not be here.

Was never meant to be.

***

With every last mote of energy I've left, I stand and drag across the chest-high stack of empty cardboard boxes from the corner I'd so neatly stacked whilst tweaking last night. I re-stack them up as tall as I can in the centre of the garage, box upon box upon box.

The twenty-metre extension cable which brings power out from the house is easy to yank free. I wind it half way in. Thick, blue, plastic-coated cable coils up and around the yellow levered bobbin in my hands. I climb atop the boxes and throw the three-pin plug over an exposed garage rafter. It dangles back down. I fasten it in place and tie the plugged end around my neck, a noose, a circle.

Do it, Séance Child.

The thing of shadows is here, around me. It grabs and forces my head up to face the sea of portraits which cover the walls. And I am lost in an ocean of ruinous burgundy and black waves. For the first time and maybe the last, I see them watching me. Falcon-eyed. All of them. They stare directly at me.

The eyes of every portrait are now mastering me. Every pair of pupils are thick, hard. and strong, and are burning into me, speaking at me without words. The pupils of myriad familiar faces chant in the silent voice of the white-eyed, black-bodied devil

122

hare: *No-one should exist, two spirits in one skin. Do it, séance girl.*

I close my eyes. A spinning zoetrope, two teardrop shapes in shades of dark and light red—both bloody—are entwined as if in battle for my soul. Loony tunes. That's all, folks.

I tighten the cord, jump up, swing my legs forward, and kick back on the stack of cardboard below. Plastic rope burns my neck as the thing that too often helps to drag me down watches on. But tonight, it does not attempt to help me down.

***

A machine beeps. Again and again. Does this mean I'm alive? Or trapped in some kind of audio torture chamber? Hell? It's not hell. I open my eyes. My boys are here. Both with red, wet eyes.

"Mummy's awake," says Sam. I try to lift my hand to take hold of his, to touch him. It takes effort, a world of effort, but my arm still works. I send a message to my toes, my calves, my legs. They move. I'm back in my body. I've no idea where I've been. I remember my portraits staring at me, judging, then I recall a sensation which sends a shudder down my hospital-bedded body. Pain kicks in. I don't want to let go of Sam's hand but I have to lift it to feel where the soreness is. My neck's on fire, shoulders too. My head is pounding.

"Don't, love. Please, leave it. Don't move the dressings." My partner takes my other hand. Sam drapes himself over me and starts to cry fresh tears.

"Where are we?" I ask.

123

My partner cut me down. I am without recollection of this. He heard something crash in the night, and concerned, came out to check on me.

"I found you just in time. What the heck were you doing?" He breaks down. They're both sobbing. I want to cry but I can't. I'm in physical agony, but otherwise, I feel borderline happy, at peace, I'm okay.

I try to recount my last moments in the garage, try to recapture the feeling, the object, the vision that made me behave the way I did, but I can't. All I can recall are the portraits and a feeling of bleakness and how someone, something had wanted me to swing from the rafters.

I feel disgusted with myself, that my partner saw me like that, dangling, limp, and my son, my young, impressionable child, saw me trollied out unconscious, white-green, to the midnight ambulance. These shards flood back. I throw up in a cardboard dish.

I hear my child weeping and this is remedy enough. Nearly dying has taught me how much I want to live.

***

I spend several weeks in this room. People checks my 'obs' relentlessly, yet I sleep better than I have in years. I don't know if it's the new medication the medics are insisting I must take and carry on with if I ever want to go home, or the fact that I appear to have reached rock bottom and the only other

124

direction I can move on is upwards, but I feel ... well.

I dress to leave. Sam and my partner are with me. Sam's drawing pictures, wants to be an artist like me. My partner tells me Sam has developed a penchant for the darker shades, for charcoal, grey and rust pastels. "What are you drawing?" I ask. He looks up but doesn't look me in the eye. "Look at me, Sam. Let me see your beautiful face."

I look at my partner who asks me not to push it. Sam muffles something: *forests, trees, the woods at night, and all the creatures that don't sleep within it,* and then, still without eye contact or looking at me at all, he speaks again, louder, "Mummy, it's gone. Your yin-yang mark. Gone." He carries on with his grim sketch. I notice each Charon's-obol-eyed owl, squirrel, and badger, wear a tight leash around their neck.

I raise a hand to my breastbone. Now my bandages are gone, all I can feel is the burn scar around my neck. I walk into the bathroom to check in the mirror. My boy speaks the truth. I turn and look at my partner who shrugs his shoulders and carries on packing my bag. Like my foggy memories of that night in the garage, memories I know intrinsically I won't miss, it's gone. My demons, my birthmark have washed away like prints in the sand. A décolletage of smooth pale skin bar a constellation of freckles, and a ring of bruising further up to my neck are all I see.

***

125

Weeks pass and things feel different. I feel different. I can sleep, nothing weighs me down, makes an infernal armchair of my chest. I paint. Every character I've met over the past few weeks appears on the wall of my gallery garage, but I don't paint out there. Sam won't allow it. Our box room has become a miniature indoor studio. I've mastered eyes which I hope doesn't devalue my work because I feel happier with each piece.

My partner hasn't once claimed victorious over the collection of medicine bottles and pill packets that now sit in our medicine cabinet. I observe my son and the artistic talent he seems to have inherited— although often a little morbid—and my heart swells. My mind speaks clarion for the first time in forever. It declares from every ounce, every cell of my body, that I'll never try to leave him, them again. I could never inflict such pain on the pair of them again.

But frustration rises to a crescendo. Although he never leaves my side, sleeps in between us every night in bed, follows me like a friendly ghost, my son still won't, can't look me in the eye. My partner says Sam's afraid to look at me, sees swirls of black and white where everyone else sees my amber irises and my pupils.

***

It's a warm Tuesday evening. I hear a knock at the door. I've been internet shopping again, whilst riding this perpetual, sleepless, upswing that is now my nearly merry life. It's a parcel addressed to Sam, something I've ordered for him.

I bring it through, sit next to him on the carpeted floor of the lounge, and push the large gift towards him. He thanks me and I feel a pang of sadness that he's opening it without a single look my way. I grab his chin, cup it in my hand, and draw his face up to look at mine. "Look at me. I'm here. I'm never leaving you, I promise." I say and his eyes are looking straight into mine for the first time since that night and his eyes are full of fear and hurt and a power, a force, that is stronger than anything the darkness has ever threatened me with. It's the overwhelming strength of a terrified love that a young child has for a parent they've witnessed dance the closest dance with death.

"But how do I know? I keep having nightmares. About you, your body. Every night. Then I feel this pushing feeling on my chest."

I bring my finger up to his lips and hush him not wanting to hear what he's about to say. I hug him in close and comfort him as his tears flow and try to hold back mine. Minutes pass which fill an eternity. I encourage him to open up the gift. He rips into the brown tape package and unfolds the flaps. An almost-smile pulls at the corners of his lips.

"Canvases. For me? Proper canvases?"

"Yes. So you can paint, express yourself. Want to go up now, do something together?"

He smiles but his eyes sink and again flit away from the direction of my loving stare. "I would Mummy, but I'm tired. Really, really tired."

It's half past three in the afternoon.

He places the canvas back down. A shadow creeps out from underneath, from within the folded cardboard packaging. It swells and grows and sits to the side of my boy. My heart thrums and not because of my balancing medication. I fear I've seen this shape before. Oh, ominous, devil-rabbit-shaped cloud of evil, what are you? It looks at me with white hole eyes and then shifts its glare directly to my son.

"Need to go to bed, Mummy. Tired," he says and rises to his feet. As he leaves the room and climbs up the stairs, I watch helplessly, frozen with dread, as this horrific creature of darkness which appears to be dressed in shadows follows him up.

I'm unable to cry or scream. Medication has me muted like a de-strung harp but inside I'm quaking with fear and shattering with worry.

It is not only my artistic skills which I've passed on to my son.

Hunger Stone (Liam A. Spinage)

There are a number of black plastic sacks in the
trunk of his car, each contains a carefully wrapped
human limb. That's probably all the information
you need to identify the chosen career of James
Patrick Devereaux.

That is, until today.

He stands on the edge of a reservoir, gripping the
handrail with a hand fully encased in a soft pigskin
driving glove. The other hand is busy dialing a
stored number on his cellphone. A pair of powerful
binoculars hang from a leather cord around his slim,
tanned neck. They sway slightly against the crisp
whiteness of his shirt. For someone who has made a
living the way he does, he looks distinctly perturbed
about something. That is, he looks perturbed for
him: it manifests only momentarily as a raised
eyebrow, a slight scowl and the call he is about to
make. Whatever the problem is, James is about to
make it someone else's problem as well as his. He's
that kind of guy.

"We got a problem." We. A problem shared is a
problem halved.

The voice at the other end of the line is muffled.
There's some shouting in the background, then a
door slams shut and the voice becomes clearer.

"Hey, Paulie here. What's up?"

He briefly allows himself another scowl since
nobody is watching. When this is over, he'll need to
have words - again - about giving names over the

129

phone. You'd think the mob would know better, but Paulie's old school.

"I need you to meet me immediately at Kensico Dam Plaza. I've sent the coordinates to your cell." No point in having a protracted conversation at this point. The problem will be obvious when Paulie gets here. James goes back to his car, closes the trunk and leans patiently against the driver's door until his guest arrives, reading the Wall Street Journal in the blazing sunshine without even raising a bead of sweat despite the heat and the impeccable tailored suit he still wears almost in defiance of it.

The same can't be said of Paulie when he arrives. He's every inch an old-style capo, three-piece Italian suit and expensive leather shoes. The suit jacket, though, is hanging over the seat of the car. Paulie - this is 'Big' Paulie, so there's just over five feet two of him - steps out, getting mud on his shoe. He curses and immediately lights a cigarette.

James sighs inwardly and makes another note to explain patiently about forensic evidence - again - at an appropriate time when Paulie won't just shout and spit in his face for five whole minutes. They've actually got more important business right now.

Paulie is perspiring profusely. Huge sweat pools are clearly visible under his arms and across his chest. He takes a handkerchief from his waistcoat pocket and mops his brow, as if that will make a difference other than to stop the sweat dripping into his eyes. His thinning hair is already plastered to his head. He wanders over as if he had all the time in the world.

"It's hot, huh?" Paulie states the obvious because he isn't much of a conversation starter and besides, he only knows who this guy is through his reputation, he's never met the famous fixer in person. He does know that he's on books for all the families in New York, that he's a serious player and not to fuck with him. But that doesn't lead to a character introduction or chit chat. He's been called here, for fuck's sake; he's not the one who should be doing the talking right now.

"97 degrees. Hottest the city has ever been. It's a little cooler out here, but it's still not good news."

"So, what am I doing here instead of standing in front of the big chest freezer in the ice cream parlor?" Paulie was irritated, running hot. It wasn't that he had anything specific to do, just that he'd rather not be doing this. He struggles to maintain composure. He s only here because if James calls, it means urgency, immediacy. At least, that's the service that was advertised. James has never called Paulie before. He hasn't needed to.

James, who was standing in front of a big freezer only a few hours ago, but for entirely different reasons, remains cool as a cucumber.

"Remember Danny Figaro? Used to sing his way through a hatchet job like he was auditioning to be an opera singer?"

"Ha, ha, yeah. I remember Danny. But he ain't a problem no more."

"I beg to differ."

Now Paulie really concentrated. If Danny wasn't dead, that was bad news. Not just because he'd be out for revenge, but because it means people have lied to him and Paulie really, really doesn't like it when people lie to him.

131

"Danny's gone, capice? Sleeping with the fishes."

"And where is it you think that fishes sleep?" James' tone is polite but inquisitorial.

"Huh?"

James raises his arms and looks around.

"Oh."

"It's been so hot and dry that on the River Po in Italy, decades-old shipwrecks have been resurfacing. We have a similar problem here. Look."

Paulie looks around for the first time, past James, over the railing and down into the reservoir. The water level is low. Dangerously low. Then it dawns on him.

"How many bodies we talking about?"

"At least six according to my records. Four of yours, one of Carlucci's and one of Moreno's. Plus, whatever or whoever got dumped here without my knowledge. If they're not already exposed - dislodged and carried to the edge - then in another couple of days, they will be. See that tunnel?"

James offers Paulie the binoculars and points at a concrete pipe just above the surface which jutted out of brown, parched rock spattered with a few hardy green weeds. Paulie nods. "That's the secondary exit overflow from the reservoir. It's supposed to provide the city with water. Now, what's wrong with this picture?"

"It's supposed to be underwater. Shit. Wait, what's that?"

"It's supposed to be *twenty feet* underwater. As to your question, I reckon that's the top half of a black

132

plastic sack not unlike the ones I have in the trunk of my car."

"Shit. Shit shit shit."

"Quite."

"Wonder who the fuck that is."

"That is what I called you here to find out."

"Shit."

***

"Here's what I don't get. This place is important, right? Supplies the city with water?" Paulie has been listening to James explain how New York's water system works for over half an hour as the two of them climb, clamber and slide their way down the steep banks of the reservoir. On the way, they'd passed different marks on the rocks which James said indicated where the water levels usually were. You could tell from the rocks and plants whether they were usually underwater or not. These rocks are slick, smooth with the gentle lapping of water over a hundred years or more. It makes it trickier to climb down and Paulie hasn't been that fit for a number of years now. Even without this heat, he'd be aching all over and wheezing right now. Even in this suffocating heat, James - who wasn't much younger but was certainly fitter - is visibly struggling and grunting.

"That's correct."

"Then why isn't it crawling with police already? Or Feds?"

James actually pauses to consider this, annoyed that he hadn't noticed the absence of law enforcement

133

himself, that he'd developed a chink in his armor that had allowed Paulie a well-placed blow. It was true that the place usually had a police presence. All the reservoir network did, even those initial lakes that were actually well beyond traditional NYPD jurisdiction. He knows this partially because three of them are technically on his payroll. They look the other way when he needs them to, but what they don't do, apparently, is tip him off when something like this happens, something which threatens his clients. He'd had to discover it himself when he arrived here. He hadn't even had the presence of mind to realize himself what the heatwave might mean to reservoir levels. He manages a scowl, mostly at his own lack of foresight rather than directed at Paulie, before rallying himself to a riposte.

"You're right. There's usually a patrol, plus manned observation points around the lake. Let's proceed while we're not being watched. We can figure out what happened to them later."

Paulie is happy enough just to have got one over on James. Now they've reached the pipe entrance, he leans against the cool concrete of the tunnel, just out of the line of direct sunlight, to catch his breath, which he does by the absurd confabulation of panting and having another cigarette. James looks cautiously around the opening and prods the muddy bank with the remains of a sapling he's hauled out of the ground on the way down. This way, he manages to fish out three plastic sacks before Paulie has recovered enough to help him.

"So, who we got?" Paulie isn't big on we, doesn't budge an inch. He is, however, merrily poking around in the mud which, despite the heat, still pools in the cool shadows just beyond the tunnel entrance. It looks a lot bigger now they're standing directly in front of it: a well-worn circular passageway of solid concrete which leads into the side of the reservoir and slightly down. It gets dark pretty quick, and Paulie is using some antique cigarette lighter to illuminate a miniature fraction of the darkness within. James tosses him a flashlight.

"This one's Joey Manzini."

"Huh. Didn't even know about him."

"You're not the only one paying for my services." Spoken out loud it sounded curt - rude, even - but Paulie supposedly already knew this. They'd all signed off on it in one of those rare moments when they had all been in the same room and nobody had immediately started shouting at each other. The good old days.

"It's definitely him. There's a serial number on the blue plastic handles of each bag, if you know where to look. Trust me, unless someone has been up here and switched body parts among different bags - after they've already been given concrete shoes and without me knowing, - it can't be anyone else."

"Hey, look at this." Paulie had been waving the flashlight around in the entrance, sending rays of light into the subterranean gloom like a kid playing with a new toy. The beam strikes a flagstone in the tunnel floor which isn't slick with slime like the others. It remains a soft, dull gray.

135

James, his identification work done for the time being, walks over. If nothing else, humor the guy. No point getting on his bad side.

"What is it?"

"Writing. In Latin. Si videries me lamentate. Huh?"

James fumbles with his phone. "Hold up a sec. I'll pop that through google translate."

"I know what it translates to. *If you see me, weep.* I just don't get it."

"It's a hunger stone. They've been spotted in the Elbe and other rivers in this year's drought." James doesn't dwell on the intensity of the Catholic upbringing necessary to translate Latin in the field. He doesn't need to because Paulie is busy tugging at the little silver crucifix around his scrawny, liver-spotted neck. "Supposedly they were used to mark desperately low river levels that would forecast famines. Odd to see one in a reservoir that wasn't constructed until the late 1800s."

Paulie doesn't miss a beat to wonder how James knows this shit either. As far as he understands it, it's literally James' job to know weird shit like this.

What neither of them know, though, is what the sign underneath the message means. It's been etched hard into the stone with a coarser instrument than the precision of the text and it looks exactly like a kid's crude crayon drawing of a branch, surrounded by smudged squiggles which look meaningless but kind of make your head hurt if you try and focus on them for too long, Paulie is finding this out the hard way while James takes photos on his phone camera.

Paulie stands, woozy, and staggers back into the sunlight where he retches a few times and then leans against the entrance again. James goes deeper, not by much, and Paulie sees a few flashes of light coming from the tunnel and a couple of scuffling noises. Then he comes out, dragging the flagstone in one hand and a small black plastic bag in the other.

"Give me a hand with this." James keeps the bag and Paulie takes the weight of the uprooted stone.

"And just what are we going to do with that?"

"Get it to an expert. Something weird is going on here and I've got a hunch that crop failure wasn't the thing the hunger stone was meant to warn people about."

"And what makes you think that?" Paulie's expression shows a modicum of curiosity, no ear and a little annoyance at having to do some heavy lifting, presumably all the way to the lip of the reservoir back to their cars.

"Call me cynical," James quips as he holds open the bin bag so Paulie can get a look, "but at a guess I'd say it's the desiccated remains of at least two NYPD officers." Paulie recoils, retches again and then gathers himself. He's glad the only thing he's carrying back to the car is a heavy stone inscribed with arcane gobbledygook.

***

They decide to take Paulie's car, on account of James' car already having most of a dead body in it. Paulie drives, naturally. James broods silently in the passenger seat. Neither of them wants to talk about what might be going on, but it's clear after a few minutes of silence that there's nothing else for them to talk about.

"So, any idea what those symbols are?" Paulie fires the opening shot.

James shakes his head. In comparison to his usual stoic-slash-pensive, this makes him positively fidgety. "Not a clue. Not my wheelhouse. I have to admit being stumped on that matter. I'm going through all the ramifications, though. Potential action plans and ways we could proceed. The original problem hasn't gone away, but we need to get this angle sorted before we can reduce ourselves to the previous scenario."

"Well, then, we got a guy. Let's go there and see what he says."

"What do you mean, you've got a guy? Does the family regularly subcontract out occult services?" James is keen to know the answer, because it's piqued his interest and it's something he could potentially add to his portfolio.

"Like I say, we got a guy. We always go to him when we get weird stuff." James actually looks hurt at this, Paulie notices. "This kind of weird stuff, I mean. Aw, you thought you were the only number on the rolodex. Dream on. You're good, but as you said this ain't your area of expertise. Time we paid a visit to someone who might be able to give us an answer."

"So where are we going? To see a priest?"

Paulie laughs, a throaty rattle that sets James' teeth on edge. "Nah, he ain't no priest. He's a chef." Now James looks intrigued, impressed even. Clearly the other experts on the books were as esoteric in their subject matters as he was.

"He'll be over in Hell's Kitchen." Paulie lights another cigarette, then realizes he has a passenger and makes the concession of rolling down the window, even though that fucks up the A/C. "I'm sure you'll get on just fine. We call him Frankie Pentangles."

***

James isn't sure what to expect when they finally arrive at Frankie's. Hell, he'd been expecting a priest at first, so anything he encounters now is going to reflect oddly on his initial hunch of what a guy who was the go-to occult expert for a mob family looked like. He isn't expecting something quite this chaotic, though. Chefs of his acquaintance - of which there were admittedly only three - keep a tidy kitchen, with every knife and cleaver in place and pristine work surfaces. What greets him when he and Paulie pass through the beaded curtain masquerading as a doorway at the end of a trash-ridden alley is exactly the opposite. The kitchen is a riot of color and growth. Strings of onions and garlic line the lintel over the curtain portal. Bottles of oil and vinegar, amongst other less savory sauces, adorn a multitude of tiny shelves which seem to have grown organically from the walls in accordance with Frankie's needs. There's only one working table surface, but it's solid white marble and big enough to take up most of the floorspace. It's covered with herbs, some of which look like they've arrived straight from the pages of the Voynich manuscript: James doesn't recognize their look or smell at all. Partially that's because there are three pans - no, cauldrons - bubbling away on the hobs, filling the kitchen with steam and the pungency of passata. Frankie is stirring these vigorously as he chants over them in Latin. James isn't sure what he's chanting, but he's pretty sure it's no prayer.

"Hey, Paulie!" Frankie looks up from his work and greets Paulie like an old friend, first wiping his hands on an apron, then using those same great meaty paws to grab both of Paulie's in an extended shake. That apron. which must be nearly as old as Frankie is, has the same well-worn appearance as Frankie's features. He looks comfortable in his own skin and boy is there a lot of that skin. Frankie towers over Paulie, but then most people do. What James notices first about Frankie is his girth - a huge pot belly leading up to at least three chins. Great jowls with wide open pores mark a friendly face, but Frankie's eyes tell a different story. James knows those eyes. What he's seen and done, he instantly assesses, is nothing to whatever Frankie has filled his days and nights with. So, despite initial appearances, James knows to take this guy seriously. He doesn't even ask about the occult symbols drawn on the other door to the kitchen. In any other circumstance James would assume those symbols were drawn in blood. Here, he's pretty sure it's spaghetti sauce. As they get talking, James realizes that to Frankie, they might as well be the same thing.

Paulie, evidently a frequent visitor to Frankie's kitchen, pours himself a large glass of red wine from a faded green bottle on the countertop next to the hob, sits down and pops a green olive in his mouth. James just stands there, a stranger in a strange land, not sure what to do with himself. Frankie carries on stirring as he and Paulie chat briefly in Italian. James gets restless, shuffles his feet and then bends over to lift up the hunger stone. The others make room for it on the table. They're just about to start looking at it when they're interrupted by two younger Italians who push their way through the beaded curtain. One of them is bleeding from the corner of his mouth; the other is holding his arm as if it's sprained. Frankie offers them both a glass of wine, which they take and a vial of what smells like garlic puree, which they take with them. Then they leave and Frankie turns around to face James.

"Eastern European gangs brought in a vampire to help secure their territory. Ain't no working with those schmucks." He looks James up and down, gauging his reaction. James doesn't budge, but inside he's full of questions, which somehow Frankie picks up on.

"Yeah, vampires exist. Yeah, garlic works. It ain't some heavenly power; I'll leave that kind of blessing to a priest. It works because it comes from the same land as the vampire. That's sympathetic magic for you. That's how myths are made, sonny."

James looks down at the stone. "So, what do we have here?" He needs time to compartmentalize what was just said, to pick apart every detail before

141

he can ask meaningful questions. And time may not be something that they have.

Frankie blows some of the dry summer dust from the top of the stone, then brushes it lightly with olive oil to clean it up. He does this with such reverence and in such silence that the only sounds in the kitchen are the sauce bubbling and Paulie's slurping. He takes a step back and
wipes his bro

"Well, this ain't good. Not good at all. Glad you brought this to my attention, Paulie." He shakes his big head, sending little puffs of flour into the air like dandruff. "The usual routines won't help so much, but I'll do what I can."

Paulie mutters a thanks while spitting out an olive pit. In the seconds of silence that follow, James realizes he's going to have to be the icebreaker.

"So, I judge from everything so far that this is designed to keep some kind of monster locked up? That monsters exist and you... err... you help fight them?" He's struggling now not to ask a thousand questions at once, so he focuses on just one more. "How do we put it back?"

The look Frankie gives Paulie says, 'where did you get this guy?' Then he turns back to James.

"Most people start off by asking what the usual routines are, you know."

"Except you just told me that the usual routines won't help much. So that's something that can wait. And believe me, I will ask that later."

Frankie nods again. "Well, this here is what you call a hunger stone, but not one that warns of a drought.

142

It means that something's hunger needs to be satiated before it can rest again. And what this thing eats…" He runs a fat finger over the little grooves full of oil on the stone, as if reading it again carefully, then looks up straight from his bloodshot, haggard eyes into James' unblinking ones. "What this thing eats is us."

James does blink though, just once, and pretends it's just from the smoke and heat of the day and the city and the kitchen. He's spooked, not because there are already dead people involved and may be more, but because he doesn't know yet how to fix this situation and that makes him uncomfortable.

"How many 'us' are we talking about?"

Even Paulie thinks this is cold and he's made more people dead than James has had hot dinners. Though as the conversation continues, that turns out to be not many hot dinners at all. He laughs nervously.

"That's why we call him Iceman, Frankie. Cool as a cucumber."

"It's already dried up at least three police officers. It may also have fed on Feds." This unintentional joke elicits a little chuckle from Paulie. "Plus, we never found all the body parts we were looking for. What I mean is, it may already be resting and we should deal with it before it gets hungry again, or wall it in if it's already satiated."

Frankie lets out a long, drawn-out breath which is so garlicky James can smell it from the other side of the table. "You'll have to memorize those odd sigils around the edge of the Elder Sign - that's the little tree branch - and reproduce them on a second stone

143

without your brain frying. What's more, you'll have to do that in situ. I'll mix up something that'll help. In the meantime, we'll need to mix something else up that I ain't got in my kitchen. I assume that either or both of you gentlemen are familiar with a cement mixer."

Paulie makes a couple of calls to what he calls his cobbler, still sipping on the wine, which visibly irritates James. Frankie, who is pounding a mixture of garlic, dried oregano and fresh-cut basil in a giant pestle and mortar, looks to bust to interrupt. Occasionally, he mutters something over them, either in Latin or Italian but James isn't sure which.

"How is that helping?" It's not that James is exasperated, so the question doesn't come out like that - it's a genuine enquiry. He does wait until Frankie has finished though.

"It's magic."

James remains silent.

"OK, I'll go into a little more detail without giving away all the secrets. It works a little like the garlic does. It'll work on Paulie here because he grew up eating this. Cooking is alchemy, y'see. You follow a certain recipe, or sometimes you have a little experiment. Either way, it produces something of lasting value. I can turn pasta into gold, metaphorically, when I serve it up and people are nourished by it - and I don't just mean physically."

Frankie wheezes a little, clearly exhausted by the physical and mental effort he was putting into this concoction. "All the little habits you learn - how to best cut up garlic, how to stir the sauce, they're like little rituals. They make the magic work. See?" He holds out a ladle for James to taste from, which he tentatively does. Frankie looks deep into him again, eager to see the reaction. When there isn't one, he's disappointed.

"Where are your people from?" On the other side of the table, Paulie finishes his drink and laughs.

"He won't say. Part of his mystique." The tone is definitely mocking. James frowns.

"What do you usually cook for yourself?" Frankie tries a different tack. Here it is, James' first visible squirm. A question he doesn't want to answer, since he lives mostly off protein shakes, energy drinks and vitamin supplements.

"Look, Paulie there, he's fortified by that wine. That wine comes from the same part of the old country his family grew up in. These connections are important. Capice?"

James gets the idea. "I'm Scots-Irish." That's what his name says, that's what he sticks to if pushed. He doesn't mention the Quebecois connection, since nobody knows his name is Devereux and that's how he wants it to stay.

"Well then, have a glass of whisky. It'll do wonders." Frankie goes to reach down to a battered white cabinet in the corner by the other door.

"I don't drink."

Both the Italians turn on him at that point. Paulie looks surprised, Frankie looks disappointed.

"Better piggy-back on our good fortune then." He opens a little cupboard above the drinks cabinet and withdraws a little cardboard box tied up with a silver ribbon. "It won't work as well, but it'll do something. Here." He thrusts the box into James' hand and sits back down.

"This thing in the tunnel is what the lore calls a flying polyp. It's invisible to the naked eye and you'd better pray you don't see it anyway. If you thought those symbols messed with your mind, you ain't seen nothing yet. Firearms will barely hurt it. You can electrocute it if you're lucky. But best just try and seal it back in with a new flagstone."

James opens the box to reveal four little tube-shaped shells of dough stuffed with cream. He looked up at Frankie.

"Those are the only shells you'll need in this fight. Trust me. Leave your gun. Take the cannoli."

They leave Frankie finishing off the last of the wine as Paulie chuckles all the way back to the car.

***

The heat hasn't diminished even though it's early evening by the time they get back to the reservoir. The stubborn sun has apparently hardly dipped an inch. They arrive at a scene that's evidently been disturbed since they were last there.

"Man, your car's been trashed." Paulie is trying not to laugh at James' misfortune, but his sick humor is tempered, mostly by the fact that James doesn't seem to care. There are heavy dents on the roof where it looks like something very heavy has landed and then sat for a while. The trunk has been utterly trashed, picked apart and left a wrangled, twisted mess of metal, the contents absent.

146

"Like a tin opener..." Paulie mutters, mostly to himself. He's scared now, probably more scared than he's been in his long, violent life and keeps looking up at the sky until he remembers that Frankie said the thing's not visible to human eyes. Then he looks even more worried.

James is busy with the rest of the scene, working out what happened and what it can tell them about their foe. If he's annoyed at the damage to his car, scared at what they might be facing or has any feelings at all, he's not showing them beyond a certain tenseness in his shoulders. That in itself might just be battle-preparedness though. James' fight-or-flight reaction is even more heavily skewed in one direction than Paulie's.

Paulie's guys have evidently delivered the cement mixer and some supplies. It also appears they left in a hurry, as evidenced by the skid marks in the dry dirt at the edge of the car park, but there's no other sign of a struggle. James takes a few photos of the car on his phone, including a couple of close ups of the giant five-toed radial footprints on the roof. He's using this to assess the size and weight of the enemy, assessing what they might be facing even though he still hopes they won't need to face it. Then he turns his mind to the pressing practicalities of the situation.

"The cement's nearly ready. Help me pour it out into a decent sized slab." James is keenly aware of their environment and the tasks ahead of them - getting the slab down the side of the reservoir before it sets properly and then this weird ritual

Frankie has primed them for. If he wasn't so focused on them then he'd be more worried that Paulie has lost some of spark and complies to his request without quips or complaint.

"Right, it's done. Now all we gotta do is get it down this pit, and quick. I don't wanna be no monster's dinner." Paulie heaves the slab up and carries it himself, carefully at the edges so as not to ruin the wet cement, which is already starting to set in the extreme heat. He's aware that James already seems to have his hands full. Two assault weapons crisscross his lean, muscled torso and there are a handful of grenades and a taser on his utility belt. Over his shoulder, James has a large bag though Paulie isn't sure what's in it, except that it doesn't look like people for a change.

They're about two-thirds of the way down when everything goes straight to hell. It starts with a strange disturbance in the air around them, like a heat haze suddenly descending on them both. It prickles their skin and makes their hair stand on end. Before they can react, there's a strange mixture of noises - a whistling of the wind, a whirring of metal blades clashing against each other, a low hum which seems to throb in the air around them. Then the winds pick up, throwing dust in their faces, scraping their skin with its heat and fury. Then there's a sudden shift in the air as the creature appears above them for a single moment. That moment is enough to drive both of these hardened men to utter panic, fear and lunacy.

There are long, thin tendrils which emanate from what James presumes is the creature's head, though this proves difficult to determine as there are several mouths across the surface of the thing's thick gray hide and each of those slavering jaws are brim-filled with teeth sharper than Frankie's knives. Long barbs also protrude from that skin, except where its form tapers down to a resemblance of a tail, though that also ends in some sort of opening the purpose of which James is keen not to discover. What passes for eyes are softly glowing, palpating growths around the principal mouth. James gets one good look at this before the dust storm blinds his vision and the sheer horror of what they face assaults his senses. He manages in that moment to reach down to his belt and grab a handgun, which he then proceeds to fire blindly, more in desperation than hope.

Paulie fares a little better. He raises the slab against his head, straining every muscle in his skinny body but protecting him from the worst of the dust storm and sparing him the bother of seeing the thing in the flesh. He continues to stagger down the side of the reservoir, hoping that James is either going to keep up or remain behind to deal with the creature. It doesn't immediately occur to him that James can presently do neither of those things. This immediate self-preservation saves him from the mental assault, but by marking himself out as the greater threat it does nothing to prevent him from the physical. The first swoop nearly knocks him off his feet. The thing is nearly four times Paulie's height and considerably bulkier. It uncoils in the air above him and dives straight down again. This time it hits home. Paulie, still managing to grip the slab he must enchant at the entrance, is knocked over and tumbles down the side of the pit, leaving James on his own.

James recovers quickly, just in time to see Paulie's hasty, forced descent through the air as he struggles to slow his fall. His initial view of the creature was so brief and so deleterious to his concentration that he hasn't been able to identify any possible weakness in the thing's body. For the first time in his life, he's starting to regret the choice of tools he's brought with him. Not that he's ready to embrace Frankie's unorthodox approach, but he'll definitely consider it if he survives the day. There's a moment of respite when he realizes the thing's attention is elsewhere, then a moment of horror when it dawns on him that he'd better get its attention back, pronto, otherwise Paulie will have no chance with the slab. He unslings an assault rifle and gets to work.

Paulie is at the cliff bottom, His shirt and waistcoat are torn to shreds and there are broad lacerations down his back from where he's plunged down the scree, blood mingling with sweat in a hundred tiny wounds. He's covered in a thick layer of dust, disoriented and winded. Down but not out. He has a thumping headache, though that's more from the mental assault of the creature than the background problems of the heat, the dust and the wounds. He fist-pumps the air to punctuate his moment of triumph. The slab is intact, the tiny jars of herbs and spices from Frankie are miraculously intact, for which he takes a moment to thank the saints. Then he orients himself and begins scrabbling around the bottom rim of the reservoir to get to the entrance of the hole. Above him, he can hear the familiar sound of gunfire. He knows from Frankie that this isn't likely to do any good, but through the brain fog he knows that's not the point. James is putting his life on the line to buy him some time. He tries to spit out the dust in his mouth, but it's too dry to have any effect. Sitting down to get his breath, he opens one of Frankie's vials - which happens to contain a good Perricone - and takes a swig.

James curses and drops the spent gun, which clatters down the cliff. Taking a moment to locate Paulie, he looks down and spots him sitting on a rock drinking something like he's on a damn picnic. Maybe it's part of the plan, maybe Paulie's just a liability at this point. The thing is still up there, somewhere, in that cloud of dust. In fact, it's only because of the dust that he can see the outline of it. He reaches around into his backpack and struggles with a side pocket until the flap opens and he pulls out his night vision goggles. That ought to even the odds. Looking through them makes no difference though, there's still only a rough outline of where the thing actually is. He swears and leaves them dangling around his neck while he plans his next move. That's when the monstrosity lets out a great shriek which makes his eardrums bleed and dives, dives, dives. It's forgotten about him and gone back to Paulie.

Paulie is spent, breathless, bleeding but his head is no longer pounding. He stands right where the

151

former stone was and has dropped the new one in place. It's quiet in here, and cool, and both of these things serve to calm him somewhat. His bloodied knuckles close in on a jar of pureed herbs which he pries open and then dips an olive branch in. Starting to recite the Latin phrases, fresh in his mind from Frankie's instruction, he thanks James for buying him some time with his life. As he starts chanting, part of him takes stock that despite his whole brain feeling like its melting from the inside out, he has become extraordinarily focused on the ritual. So much so that two things that should occur to him pass him by completely. Firstly, that with patterns swirling round in his vision, he wouldn't notice if the horror came up right behind him now. Secondly, that what he's doing at the moment is effectively trapping the flying polyp outside the tunnel rather than inside. Only when he can see James in his peripheral vision, frantically waving his arms and shouting, does he realize either of these and by then he's so involved he can't stop.

James beckons at Paulie frantically, but to no avail. He can't see the monster, can't feel its presence at all and that worries him, but not as much as what Paulie's up to. How intelligent is that thing anyway? Does it realize that Paulie's about to accidentally grant it eternal freedom from its tunnel? Is that what it wants? He'd managed to get a tracker on it earlier with a lucky shot but even the screen output showing its location far above them is blurry and indistinct. He'll need to attract its attention again and somehow get it back inside the tunnel, past the

152

both of them, without either of them getting hurt. None of the various mouths and tendrils and barbs and coils on the thing look like something he wants to get bitten, stung or hit by. He's about to go back to the tunnel mouth when something comes crashing down on him. It's not the polyp, though. It's his car.

Paulie is lost in the moment, tracing arcane glyphs into the drying cement with an olive branch and chanting phrases he's only heard once before which nevertheless seem to exit his lips with perfect clarity. He's never felt such serenity before. It leaves him breathless. It leaves him vulnerable.

Only a few seconds after the car crashes in front of James' eyes, knocking him to the tunnel floor mere inches from Paulie, the air starts to vibrate again and the thing slowly congeals into the air in front of him. James has only one close-up weapon, but he figures it could irritate the thing long enough to make him the primary target again. He whips out the taser and blasts it straight at one of the masses of eyes surrounding the central maw. There follows the most execrable screech he's ever heard and all the tendrils whip around blindly. Three of them make contact with his bare arm and leave stinging welts on his flesh.

That got its attention.

Once it has stopped thrashing, it pulsates and writhes again, sending a hot blast of air and a wretched hollering whoop into the tunnel. James can't see it now, but he knows when it's getting close to him because he's used the one thing that he picked up at Frankie's which he figured might

153

actually be of practical use. Even in the gloom of the tunnel, he can make out approaching five-toed prints in the flour he's strewn around the entrance. Waving a flare in one hand, he's pretty sure he's got its attention. It barrels past Paulie and heads straight at him.

"Si videries me lamentate." Paulie speaks the last words of the chant, the warning that will tell people not to disturb this place again. He's barely conscious now, not from any wounds but from the pressure on his mind and the disturbances in his peripheral vision which resemble the remnants of a really bad LSD trip. But he holds on long enough to draw the branch of the Elder Sign onto the slab. There's an unholy wail from deeper in the tunnel which he can just make out before he passes out. It's done.

James reaches Paulie only moments later. His arms aren't strong enough to lift him because the sting of the tendrils have done their work and he can't even lift his gun. But he can drag Paulie out to the sunlight. Those last few moments of that battle, where the thing manifested long enough to stare directly at him, all its eyes ablaze with millennia of blind rage and hatred, those moments just before he managed to slide beneath it and skid across the tunnel floor, will stay with him for a while, but for now there is only silence and the lingering heat of the setting sun.

They don't talk to each other at all on the way back. Paulie drops him off at a bar in Queens without even realizing where it is that James has asked to be dropped off. It's genuinely amazing that he managed to grip long and strong enough on the wheel to get them both back to the city.

***

James goes straight into the long, low, nearly empty bar, ignoring the few disapproving looks he gets at his appearance. When he finally stops shaking, he manages to clean himself up a little in the restroom and then stares at himself in the mirror for what seems like an eternity. Then he goes back into the bar and orders a whisky. His hand grasps the glass with the loose grip of the utterly unfamiliar as he raises it to his mouth in a solitary toast to success.
"It works, doesn't it?"
Frankie sits down next to him. James doesn't even know how he's got here, then remembers Paulie must have told him.
"It's starting to."
"Uh-huh."
"Tell me more. I want to know everything."

155

The Mischief Queen (Sandra Stephens)

"She is deeply concerned
With the ways of the mice
Their behavior's not good
And their manners not nice"

~ T.S. Eliot

You can learn a lot by paying attention, even if you are only eleven years old. My name is Victoria Amelia Mast and I am actually eleven and three quarters years old, though on paper I sound a good deal older owing to my voracious reading and in person I look a good deal younger owing to my condition and my very slight stature. *Voracious* means having a very eager approach to an activity.

What I lack in size I make up for in vocabulary. I have a large vocabulary on account of my reading books. Even children's fiction books are written by real adults, which is how I've come to know so many adult words. I first read the word 'assassin' in the story of Pinocchio. *Assassin* is another word for murderer. I try to learn at least one new word every day.

I live at 7191 Stiles Street in Charlestown which is the oldest house in the oldest neighborhood in Boston which is also known as the Cradle of Liberty. My mother lives here when she is not busy trying to find a husband. I see her only once a fortnight and sometimes less than that. A *fortnight*

156

is a period of two weeks. There are twenty-six fortnights in a year.

I attended school until fourth level but because of my condition I am now tutored at home by Professor Vreem who comes every Monday, Tuesday and Wednesday from nine in the morning until four in the afternoon. Professor Vreem says I am at least three levels ahead of other children my age. That's because I dedicate an entire day of the school week - Thursday - to reading. Readers are leaders, Professor Vreem says.

I am half British as my father George Basil Mast is from Harrowden, Bedfordshire which is in England. My mother says that being half British accounts for my locution which some find peculiar. My father disappeared when I was too young to remember him. To *disappear* means to vanish from sight.

I have only one memory of my father. In this memory I am on the floor playing on the rug in his study. Mother is there but she has her back to me and to father as he fastens a necklace about her neck. There is a fire in the fireplace which makes father's blonde hair glow pale golden yellow, especially compared to mother's black hair. How I wish I had inherited father's yellow hair and blue eyes. I prefer light eyes, since mine are dark.

Later when Mother kissed me good night the pendant dangled above me, round and gold like a moon with letters on it. I cannot tell you what letters because in this memory I am too young to read. I asked mother if she has the necklace still and she told me I was dreaming; that Father never gave her jewelry. I told Mother that I never dream because of

157

my condition and why would I dream of a different rug in the study but everything else the same as it is now and she said in a very cross voice what a strange child I am and to run along. To be *strange* is to be unusual or surprising in a way that is unsettling or hard to understand.

I heard Cook say to Housekeeper my father deserted us. To *desert* is to abandon in a way that is disloyal or treacherous, like soldiers in a war.

The only things my father left behind are his book collection and the house at 7191 Stiles Street. Except it is not really my father's house but the house of his mother, who was my grandmother though I have never met her. She disappeared one day when my father was too small to remember her, the same way that my father disappeared when I was almost too small to remember him. Grandfather says it is a case of the acorn falling not far from the tree. I wonder if I too shall one day be a Mast who has disappeared, with an unlucky child who cannot remember me? To disappear is to cease to be visible.

Grandmother willed her house to father and in the will states that her husband - that's grandfather - and his descendants - that's father, and me - are to live in the house and be provisioned for until their deaths. To *provision* is to supply with food and drink. The will doesn't say anything about mother, naturally, because grandmother died before mother was born. Grandfather called this a technicality and forbids mother to freeload on his dear departed wife's generosity. A *technicality* is a point of law or a small detail of a set of rules.

158

Mother lives at different hotels, always the nicest with suites of rooms and silk pillowcases and velvet tapestries and bidets made of marble.

Mother says the same thing every time she comes for a visit: *When your grandfather passes maygodforgiveme by law the house becomes ours.* She always sounds happy at the idea even though she spends so little time here. She says just wait, some day she will come home with a provider who can take us on travels and shopping and to restaurants and not have to stay in this drafty haunted old house all the time. Because of my condition I am trepidatious at the notion of travel but if we dine out I can wear my best red pinafore. To be *haunted* is to have ghosts.

When I ask Mother where we will travel to she laughs and says Anywhere we want, the world will be our oyster! Cook served oysters for dinner once, on Grandfather's eightieth birthday. I did not like them. There was a sauce of butter covering a nasty thing that looked like an infected boil Cook once had on her foot, after lancing it. Grandfather became angry at me for not eating the infections and called me a spoiled brat. To be *spoiled* means to be harmed in character by being treated too leniently or indulgently.

***

Grandfather cannot leave his wheelchair and spends much of his time in his bedroom suite on the first floor shouting at Cook to get him his heart pills which are very tiny and are stored in a cunning little

159

amber bottle I should quite like to have. The dining room and sitting room are also on the first floor. A housekeeper comes once every week, but she cleans only the first floor ever since climbing three flights of stairs became too difficult for her knees.

It falls to me to clean my own room as well as the schoolroom which I do once every week on Fridays. I wash the blackboard, sweep the floor and dust Professor Vreem's desk, also the shelves that hold my school books and the windowsill inside and out. I finish by clapping the erasers in the garden. I do this even if they have no chalk dust in them, because everyone expects to see me do it.

I have noticed that while I am doing things people *expect*, they go back to not paying attention to me. If they do not see me do what they expect they say the same things always: *Did you clean the schoolroom today?* and *Stay out of mischief, now.* A *mischief* is playful misbehavior or troublemaking none of which I am likely to experience due to my condition and the fact that I do not have any playmates.

I am a very tidy person by nature. I surmise that I inherited this quality from my father. To *surmise* is to suppose that something is true without evidence. When I asked mother if father was tidy, she laughed and called him a Neat Nick. This annoyed me because my father's name was not Nick but George. Cook says father's father who is my Grandfather is also named George so my father was known by his second name, Basil which I must say I like better than George. Basil is a member of the mint family.

I always make sure Father's study on the third floor is neat as a pin, much like mine. Mother could not be more different; on her visits she always leaves her clothes all over the chairs and floor and eats in her bed and leaves the trays on her quilt with food all over the china dishes. She locks the door to her room when she is gone, so I cannot clean it for her.

***

Today whilst cleaning the schoolroom I heard a squeak. It was a small sound, so small I had to stand very still to hear it. It is strange how much noise there is in silence. The wind was blowing and branches scratched the windows like fingernails. There was the creaking sound Cooks says is the wood of the house shrinking in the cold. There was the distant sound of grandfather coughing down in the sitting room. Then I heard it again.

"I hear you," I called. I kept my voice soft so Cook wouldn't hear. "But where are you?"

The squeak came again, and then again. After a bit of a search I was able to locate the source: a tiny pink thing lying on the floor at the very back of the room. At first I thought it was a pencil eraser but when it moved I saw it was a tiny live thing, with four legs and closed eyes. It was no longer than my pinky finger and could barely lift its head.

It squeaked again, perhaps sensing me looming above it. To *loom* is to appear as a shadowy form, especially one that is large or threatening.

I hurried to my room, removing my shoes so that Cook would not hear me. In my stocking feet I

161

fetched the jewelry box Mother presented me for my last birthday. It is empty except for the little ballerina who sleeps when the lid is closed and twirls to music when the lid is opened. I lined it with a handkerchief so that it was now a little bed. I was very careful as I lifted the tiny pink thing into the bed.

I have no idea what it could be, or where it came from. Professor Vreem might know, but he will not be back until next week, after spring holiday concludes. Perhaps I tracked it in from the garden. I cannot ask Cook or Grandfather, they are almost certain to intervene and take it from me. To *intervene* is to come between so as to prevent or alter a result or course of events.

It was so very weak and so small, but I felt a tiny movement when I wetted my pinky finger in water and pressed to its wee mouth. I twisted a handkerchief and drenched the tip in milk which it sucks with the tiniest little movements of its cheeks. It seems to be taking nourishment and I feel encouraged it will survive. For now it resides within the jewelry box, the ballerina standing guard. I keep the box in an open drawer in the nightstand next to my bed.

***

Grandfather says children are a consternation that should be seen and not heard and if I speak he gets very red in the face and has to take a tiny pill to stop his heart from being angry. A *consternation* is a feeling of dismay.

162

When mother is at home it is wonderful but Grandfather shouts even more than usual. It makes me so anxious the only thing I can do is stare at him without a sound until he shouts *Don't you look at me you little freeloading freak.* To *freeload* is to take advantage of other people's generosity without giving anything in return. Mother says that Grandfather has dementia and cannot be blamed for the things he says. I think he dislikes the fact that my eyes do not always quite look in the same direction. People never know which eye to fix on when they speak to me so they generally would rather not.

***

It seems to be getting bigger, though it is hard to tell. After two days I can see little ears. Its eyes are still closed and now there is a darkish stripe down the middle of its naked pink back which I hope does not mean it is rotting, the way the fish Cook brings back from market sometimes do.

***

My bedroom and my mother's bedroom are on the second floor and my schoolroom is on the third floor. Every room on the third floor except my schoolroom is closed up with the furniture covered in sheets, like ghosts. There is no heat in the winter and the fireplace is never used as Grandfather says wood is too expensive to waste heating two whole

163

floors for a child the size and attractiveness of a drowned rat to just sleep and study.

One of the rooms on the third floor is my father's study. It is meant to be kept locked at all times but I have filched the housekeeper's key. To *filch* is to pilfer. One of the walls of the study is entirely bookshelves filled with books. My father's book collection contains books by many English mystery and suspense writers such as Agatha Christie and Sherlock Holmes and P.D. James, who I learned quite accidentally is not a man but a woman and so required reading all of the books a second time with this new information.

It comes as a constant surprise to me that things are not always as they seem which Mother says is part of my condition. Even words cannot be completely trusted to stay themselves, one is always finding out a word has more than one meaning and not only that the meanings might not even have anything to do with each other!

Looked at one way, to be *odd* is to be different from what is usual or expected. But odd also means having one left over as a remainder when divided by two, as I am the remainder of my divided Mother and Father. *Haunted* does not only refer to ghosts, it also means to show signs of mental anguish or torment.. And *mischief* is not just about misbehavior, it is also the word for a gathering of six or more rats! This makes me feel cross, for how can one ever know what one is talking about when word meanings can slip away and replace themselves?

164

***

I have been feeding it every two hours. It looks like a tiny pig with a tiny pig tail though that is quite impossible, according to the Encyclopedia Britannica a newborn pig will weigh two pounds at birth. This creature is smaller than my smallest finger so naturally I have begun calling him Pinky. Perhaps he is a fairy pig which is not something I would have believed existed but one must believe the evidence of one's own eyes as Mr. Watson of the Sherlock Holmes stories says, and I agree.

***

Father's study smells of dust and wood and air that is never breathed and books with pages turning yellow like Grandfather's teeth. It is quiet as graves, a good condition to read in. When I read father's books I don't feel so odd as many of the detective characters have peculiarities. Today I am reading A Case of Identity in which a woman lives on her inheritance and is engaged to be married to a man who has disappeared which turns out to be an easy case for Sherlock Holmes while Dr. Watson was mystified.

I have read sixty six mysteries by Miss Agatha Christie, plus fifty six Sherlock Holmes stories, my favorite being The Speckled Band because the speckled band turned out to be a snake an uncle has trained to kill his nieces before they marry so he can keep their inheritance.

I've read thirty two stories by Miss Patricia Wentworth that feature a governess named Maud Silver who becomes a detective. I read each book only once as I do not like the name Maud, it sounds like the name of a plain looking woman.

But I quite like the name Wentworth! It sounds very proper and well-to-do. *Proper* means exactly correct. If my mother were called Wentworth I think she might have found a proper husband by this time. I think the names of things can be very revealing.

My very favorite books are the Encyclopedias Britannica. *Britannica* is the Latin word for Britain. In my father's study there are 24 volumes of encyclopedias with green leather covers stamped with gold letters GBM. I have read all the volumes at least once and the ones with copper plate illustrations twice, with the illustrations depicting the human body with the skin flayed back to reveal the organs being my favorite.

***

It has only been a week since I found Pinky and already he is the last one I talk to at night and the first one I say good morning to. There can be no doubt he is growing. The skin of his head has become quite dark, as though he has been stained with shoe polish. His movements are stronger now, especially when I talk to him. When he squeaks, I stroke his back with my fingertip and he goes to sleep.

I wish Mother would come home more often but it is important that she find a husband. I asked Mother couldn't she live here with me until the next husband joins us and she said that while she would love nothing more, Grandfather would spoil any chance of her landing a good match.

I asked Mother if Grandfather didn't exist and she didn't need a husband could we live here at 7191 Stiles Street together, and she called me a darling child and said that of course she'd love nothing more, just two women together against the world and not a husband in sight, what could be nicer.

When she speaks to me Mother's voice is bright and cracks like a mirror and when there are enough cracks I shall be able to make out what is being hidden.

***

Pinky is now covered with fur, his head with a dark hood and his body white and with a long black stripe down the middle of his back. He has the most delicate curly whiskers! He looks quite different from when I found him and I remembered an illustration in the Encyclopedia that looks much like Pinky looks now, under the entry *rattus rattus*, which is also called a house rat or sometimes a roof rat and even a ship rat! I am glad Pinky is safe in a house. I have always hoped to sail in a ship someday but it is not likely owing to my condition.

Baby rats are called pups; male rats are called bucks and females are called does. The entry goes on for more than two pages and is very informative. Based on the illustrations provided I have determined that Pinky is a buck.

The good thing about books is how a reader can learn everything the character knows in the story. For example in thirty one of Agatha Christie's stories, like *The Pale Horse,* someone dies of poison. The Encyclopedia Britannica says Miss Christie learned all about poison from being a nurse during the war.

Once I gave Cook **They Do It With Mirrors** and told her it was one of my favorite stories which it would be if Cook served Grandfather a dinner of strychnine meatloaf with belladonna gravy and cyanide tea so that mother and I could live here together. Of course I knew she would do no such thing but if she did no one would ever know because Grandfather is very old and I would never tell. I made a crease on the page with the words *Poison has a certain appeal* but everyone stayed alive after dinner that night and when Cook returned the book she said she preferred romance novels and that I should run along and stay out of mischief.

***

Pinky has opened his eyes and looks at me with the sweetest expression. Perhaps he wonders why his mother is such a giant like me! He will lick the tip of my finger or nibble my fingernail with his tiny hand touching me with such daintiness it is hard to believe that soon he will be able to chew through concrete, wood, and cinder blocks. According to the encyclopedia entry a rat's teeth never stop growing which means if Pinky does not keep chewing his teeth will get too long to eat and then he'd starve. It hardly bears thinking about and I have made a solemn vow to Pinky to keep him safe from his own teeth.

I have begun sneaking small bits of bread from my dinner plate to my pinafore pocket, and feeding them to Pinky. He shows a good appetite for something beside the milk handkerchief. He especially likes scraps of meat and grows daily. Soon he will find the jewelry box a bit cramped but for now he explores the sides with his little hands and squeaks adorably for more meat.

***

I do believe Pinky knows his name! When I call out Pinky he stands and whuffles his whiskers at me. To whuffle is snuffle with whiskers and there is no point in looking that up for I have invented it and Pinky likes it and that is what matters.

***

When the jewelry box became too small Pinky climbed out of it onto my pillow and cuddled into my hair in the space between my ear and shoulder (a place I have begun to think of as my rolder). I stroked him gently until he fell asleep and then held very still for fear any move could crush him and hoping that my heart beating for joy at the feeling of

169

his tiny breathing next to my cheek would not disturb him.

I have a confession to make. The first morning after Pinky slept like this I quite forgot, standing and walking to the bathroom, only to hear a desperate squeaking and see poor little Pinky hanging on to the end of my sleeping braid for dear life. I quickly rescued him and apologized over and over as I stroked his little head. To think I could have hurt or even killed Pinky with my carelessness fills me with a terrible feeling of sadness and dread. We both had some milk to calm down.

***

To make sure he stays safe I have taken to carrying Pinky around with me everywhere I go. He nestles perfectly in my pocket or rolder behind a curtain of my hair. During my school lessons he naps or sits quietly and Professor Vreem has no inkling that he is teaching not one but two students. An inkling is a suspicion.

***

The Encyclopedia Britannica says rats are very intelligent and even without an encyclopedia it is easy to see for myself that this is true. When the coast is clear I make a clicking sound with my tongue and Pinky will poke his little head out the top of my pinafore pocket and whuffle his whiskers at the sights and smells of the first floor. He is always very curious but when someone approaches

170

I click twice and he pops out of sight quicker than quick.

At dinner when Grandfather begins to shout, I will slip my hand in my pocket and stroke Pinky and this makes me feel less anxious.

***

Yesterday I had the fright of my life but it has been followed by the nicest surprise. While cleaning the schoolroom I looked up just in time to witness Pinky disappearing into a crack between the wall and the baseboard! I called and called but Pinky was gone. The crack did not look wide enough for Pinky to fit and inside was so dark I had to fetch a candle, but Pinky did not re-appear, not even when I announced I was going to the garden to clap erasers, something I know Pinky likes by the way he pokes his head out of my pocket and whuffles.

I sat at the hole for more than two hours and now here I sit alone in my bedroom, no Pinky in his drawer to read to and say goodnight to. I left the light burning all night long and cried myself to sleep but I knew as soon as I woke up that my hair was just hair and not a cozy nest for Pinky. I used the opportunity to wash it for the first time since finding Pinky on the schoolroom floor and found some of the strands have fused together so they seem like little ropes of hair that reminded me of Pinky's tail and caused me to cry anew at the loss of my only friend.

After breakfast I went immediately to the schoolroom with a variety of foods hidden away in my pockets (the light and empty feel of my Pinkyless pocket is truly terrible) and set them all about the dastardly crack. Dastardly means wicked and cruel. Then I sat very quietly nearby and waited to see if Pinky would appear at the smell of his favorite foods including bits of roast of beef, some cooked oats sweetened with honey, last night's buttered dinner roll of which I took only a bite and small round slices of roasted carrots and potatoes.

I sat completely still in the empty schoolroom and waited for Pinky to appear. At first I thought I must have dozed off in the quiet because when I opened my eyes I had to rub them to make sure I was not seeing things.

There, nibbling at the food, were three little Pinkys! I closed my eyes very tight and opened them again to be sure I wasn't still sleeping and there they were, three pups with black and white fur and the dearest little pink noses and hands. After a moment I detected the one eating beef was my own Pinky; the nibbler at the dinner roll had a long black stripe like Pinky's but was much narrower, and the third had a crescent shaped spot on its lower back. Soon, another pup popped out of the crack, this one completely black, and then two more, both black and one with a white foot.

In all, I counted five new pups. They made quick work of the food I had brought and when it was all gone, leaving not even a crumb, they disappeared into the gap in the wall one by one until there was only a tail sticking out and just as I wondered if it was Pinky's the tail disappeared too. It was all quite amazing and hard to take in - one would never suspect six baby rats had been eating a feast just moments before. Certainly neither Professor Vreem nor I suspected Pinky had five littermates just inches away from me in the school room three days a week.

Later that night Pinky returned to my room with me and slept in his drawer and I cried a little with happiness. It's funny isn't it - I woke up crying without my only friend, and fell asleep crying with joy at finding five new friends. Life is very much more interesting now than it used to be.

***

Mother came home for the annual visit by Mr. Richfield, the executor of Grandmother's will. Pinky and I watched from the school room window as Mother came up the sidewalk, from our view her hat looked like a black boat with a black feather for a sail.

Mr. Richfield is very old, older even than Grandfather. For the past three years he has brought with him an assistant, Mr. Archer, who is much younger with blonde hair that he combs straight back from his very tall forehead. Mr. Richfield always refers to me as the young Miss Mast, but Mr. Archer calls me Miss Victoria which I like better. Mother always tries to exclude me from these meetings because of my condition but Mr. Richfield says it-is-his-sworn-and-legal-duty-as-executor-of-the-Mast-estate-to-ensure-the-health-and-wellness-of-all-legatees (legatees being me and Grandfather).

I always wear my navy wool pinafore and black patent shoes and stand very still while Mr. Richfield looks me and my report card over with his little round spectacles. Being looked at makes my skin itch but with Pinky in my pocket I find it easier to endure.

Mr. Richfield said the same things he always says, that Professor Vreem speaks highly of me and to stay out of mischief, which almost made me laugh (but instead I just whuffled and took great delight in Mr. Richfield's look of surprise). If only he knew that a mischief was watching *him*!

Of course the mischief watches me too, which is how I know they see what I see, which is that at each of these meetings, as sure as Mr. Richfield will say Professor Vreems speaks well of his prize student - meaning me - Mother and Mr. Archer will each take a turn excusing themselves from the room, leaving me staring at Mr. Richfield who will nod off almost immediately. His snores are almost as loud as the grandfather clock which ticks like a voice that says *I see, I see*.

Mother returns to the room from these little absences in a rush of perfumed air and a flurry of cashmere and silk, her cheeks red as if she'd painted them. Mr. Archer returns always and only after Mother has retaken her seat. His eyes are downcast, his hair is raked by visible comb marks and his slight mustache appears damp, as if recently washed, or kissed. I know what a kissed mouth looks like; I've seen the cook's assistant kiss the butcher's delivery boy, from my window above the alleyway with the delivery door.

174

Mother says that Mr. Archer is very kind, and that every lady needs a Mr. Archer.

**

I have determined that two of the rat pups are bucks like Pinky, while three are does. The doe with the crescent marking I will call Maude. The third black and white is Arthur. The large black is Sam, the medium black is Montague and the smallest black is Patricia.

When it is lesson time on Fridays I line them up according to size, smallest to the largest so that they are Maude, Patricia, Montague, Pinky, Arthur, Sam. I have made a little song of their names as I do the morning roll call for which the mischief stands just as I do for Professor Vreem. They drop to all fours after I clap and call to take our seats and begin the lesson. They are very fast learners with a keen sense of humor and I am proud that Pinky is by far the quickest to respond to new signals and show the others the way. He has grown so much since the day I found him, now so robust when it did not even seem certain he would survive the first night. To be robust is to be vigorous.

Maude-Patricia-Montague, Pinky-Arthur-Sam! I hum it while I go about cleaning the schoolroom and clapping the erasers. Cook heard me and for once did not tell me to stay out of mischief and even gave me a slice of pumpernickel bread with butter for a treat. I ate half of it and stowed the rest in my pocket, where Pinky abides. To abide is to dwell.

175

I could not believe it when I returned to the schoolroom to find that Pinky had not taken even a single nibble until the rest of the mischief could enjoy it with him. It is funny to me that on the one occasion Cook failed to warn me about staying out of mischief I should find myself in the company of one!

**

Most of the time life at 7191 Stiles Street is very routine, which Mother has always said is good for someone with my condition. I have taken to doing my reading on Thursdays in the schoolroom with Pinky and his friends, who eat the food I bring for them and listen to any readings I have been assigned. This week I am reading Vanity Fair by Mr. William Makepeace Thackeray. I do not like the sound the name Thackeray makes in my mouth but I quite like the character Becky Sharp who wants only to find a rich husband and live in peace just like mother.

While reading I will click for Pinky to come and take a bit of food from my hand. Today when I clicked to my happy surprise the entire mischief came to my hand. I gave everyone a bit of food and they whuffled their whiskers at me in the most adorable way. Then I had an idea and made the double click which is my signal for Pinky to get out of sight. Imagine my astonishment as they all whisked out of sight, each one scurrying in a different direction so fast that a glance out the window and I would have missed their presence entirely.

I sat there in the empty schoolroom that was not empty at all and felt the strangest sensation that I do not know how to describe, just that it is somehow wonderful knowing Pinky and friends were nearby, unseen but seeing, ready to come to my aid at the sound of a click.

**

At dinner I have taken to wearing a snood to hide the condition of my hair, which is perfectly suited for a Pinky-sized friend to ride around on my rolder but can only be brushed with great difficulty. A snood is a type of hood or hairnet that keeps hair in place.

Tonight at dinner there was the best news ever: Mother will be coming home next week and so soon after her last visit! Her note said she has a surprise for me and I became excitable and spilled my milk, making Grandfather angry. It took Cook nearly an hour to calm him and find his little pill bottle and give him a pill but I did not mind taking my dinner to my room, where I let Pinky perch on the edge of my plate and eat with me as I told him about Mother and how beautiful she looked the last time I saw her in her red coat with the fur collar and a big black hat decorated with peacock feathers.

When it was time to go to bed there was Pinky in his little drawer looking up at me, whiskers whuffling away. I kissed him many times and though I am very clumsy because of my condition I

177

even managed to dance around the room with Pinky on my shoulder holding on to my hair ropes. I cannot wait for mother to meet Pinky!

***

We always read a story before bed. At first it was just me reading aloud and Pinky listening, either snuggled on my rolder or as is the case more and more lately in his own little drawer that he has made soft and comfortable. Lately Maude and Arthur have come to join us and sometimes Montague. I've even seen Big Sam once or twice, always when I am reading Sherlock Holmes. I know it's Sam because he likes to sit listening right where the lamp light stops.

Now we are reading The Crooked House by Agatha Christie which is one of my favorites because I would never have thought that a child like myself could ever accomplish a murder. The dead man in the story is a rich Grandfather who many family members will inherit from so any one of them could be the killer. But the killer is none other than Josephine, a girl very nearly my age who reads detective stories just like me. She almost gets away with it because everyone thinks the killer is an adult with something to gain when in fact the killer is an ugly girl who is angry at her Grandfather.

Not paying for ballet lessons is a silly reason to kill anyone but perhaps she was lonely and her only friends were in ballet class in which case I shouldn't like to be kept away from my only friends. I admire Miss Christie for her very good imagination because

Crooked House is a story I could never have thought up myself, even though I am just like Josephine except for the ballet lessons.

***

The mischief grows each day. There are eleven now at lessons and though I never see them during my own lessons, I can picture them quietly assembled on the other side of the wall while Professor Vreem instructs me. Sometimes in the dining room I have the strongest sense of being watched and it gives me such a wonderful feeling.

When I must read aloud for Professor Vreem I always talk in my Victoria Amelia Mast voice but when I read aloud at bedtime I do my best to change my voice to match the characters and I am getting quite good at it if I do say so myself. When Pinky stays in his drawer sometimes Montague or Maude and the others will climb up to my rolder and I wake in the morning with a head full of mischief. I love to hold up my silver hand mirror and see all of my friends peeking out from my hair and though I know I am thought ugly, I cannot but say they make me almost beautiful.

***

The School of Victoria Mast is gaining in reputation. Towards the end of today's lesson Big Sam jumped down from the desk although I did not click at him. Before I knew it, out from the crack between the baseboard and the wall popped five

179

mature pups I have never noticed before, three of them black like Sam and two brown. The two brown were larger even than Sam and with short tails. They all looked at me and then Sam clicked at me three times, which is the signal I use when I have brought food to share. He even nipped my fingernail to make his meaning clear, the sound exactly like a clippers will make when trimming the nail. I feel certain he did not intend to hurt or scare me.

***

I snuck down to the kitchen and put together a plate of bits and bobs from the refrigerator and pantry that Cook would not notice. Everyone ate with good appetite, and then friends new and old all settled down around me for the evening story which tonight was The Adventure of the Sussex Vampire.

***

I have named the new blacks Irene, Mycroft and Mrs. Hudson, and the browns Moriarty and Lola. Tomorrow we will conduct a review of all click signals. When Mother arrives it will be more important than ever that we keep quiet. Though I am proud that I never have to remind everyone of this, they are all naturally quiet and have a few times alerted me before someone suddenly enters a room, popping out of sight just in time.

***

180

My lessons from Professor Vreem continue, as do my lessons to the mischief which has grown so that we must open the window during class time so that visitors on the roof can hear. There are quite a lot of them but they make almost no sound. They may peep out when Cook has her head turned, to make me smile, but otherwise they are never detectable though I know they follow me about the house during the day. Once, they brought the erasers down to the garden and I looked all about the schoolroom and was quite puzzled where they could be. Cook found them and gave me the strangest look and I kept a solemn face though I could hear their laughter inside the chimney and behind the walls, it is very like the laughter of fairy people, or so I imagine.

**

The greatest shock of my life, Pinky is not a buck like I thought but a doe through and through. You might wonder at my certainty given my initial error but in this case I feel confident for you see Pinky became a mother last night, giving birth to ten pups! Each of the pups is pink and as small as the first joint of my finger, with eyes closed exactly like Pinky when I first found her.

To see Pinky nurse her babies is the happiest sight. I had a mad urge to throw open the window and shout the news and run to the garden and tell everyone that passes by, Pinky is a mama! She licks the pups with the tiniest little licks and with such care checks

181

them all over and lets me pet each one with my tiniest finger. You were just this size when I found you, I told Pinky.

Sometimes she will still climb into my hand and curl there like old times and I find it very touching and hereby make my most solemn vow to protect Pinky's babies like they were my own, which in a way they are.

***

Tonight Mother arrived in time for dinner and looked very beautiful at the dinner table, her naturally black hair has been colored red and it shone in the lamplight like a waterfall of blood. At such moments I could burst with pride that she is my very own mother. She took some wine and seemed almost to glow with happiness and even laughed at Grandfather's imprecations. An imprecation is a spoken curse.

When Grandfather said we are all whores little Montague stood up to peek over the edge of my pocket and make a squeak almost as if he meant to protect me. It was very quick and no one saw but Grandfather who began shouting with spit on his lips and pointing at my pocket. He started choking with his tongue poking out like a dead toad until Cook rushed in and gave him one of his tiny heart pills. By then Montague was safely out of sight. A *whore* is a prostitute. When I asked Housekeeper what a prostitute is she only said 'hush child. '

I wanted so much to introduce Mother to Pinky, but when I went to her room she said through the door

182

she is going to bed early and tomorrow we will have a proper visit. I went up to the schoolroom and taught everyone the newest five click signals I have made up. We are now up to forty three click signals. For a treat I read aloud one of my favorites, The Clock Strikes Twelve by Patricia Wentworth which is a book about a family who murders their old patriarch after he says terrible things about his own family members.

It is astonishing that Grandfather, who I have always feared, is himself afraid of little Montague, a fact that has given me an inkling of how to help Mother. Rats are so intelligent and understanding and brave it's hard to believe anyone could ever be afraid of them.

***

Grandfather has died. It happened at lunch. He stood from his wheelchair and grabbed his chest and then fell forward onto the table. Cook came running into the room. Grandfather slid onto the floor. His mouth opened and closed just like the fish that Cook gets at the market. His lips turned blue and his hand was sticking up like a bird claw into the air.

Cook ran out of the room to bring his tiny heart pills and call the doctor. I leaned over Grandfather on the floor. I know he saw me because I said to him very slowly and clearly' Blink if you can hear me 'and he blinked. I clicked and Montague and Patricia peeked out from behind my hair and whuffled at Grandfather. Grandfather made choking noises and seemed to stop breathing. Then I double clicked and they popped back into hiding. Cook came running back into the room, having found the amber bottle where Patricia hid it.

While they were busy taking Grandfather away I popped down to the dining room to retrieve his uneaten lunch. There was no sign Grandfather had been alive and shouting and keeping me and mother apart just hours before. The mischief left no trace anywhere, not in the folds of draperies or behind china in the banquet or under the table. You would never guess how once Cook had left the room they popped out at my click signal and ran about the room and even across the headrest of Grandfather's wheelchair. At my click signal and the whole mischief assembled on the table stood as one. I was so proud; it was such a sight to see. Grandfather stood too. Then he fell to the floor and the mischief disappeared at the sound of my click signal and no one was the wiser for their hidden presence. Except Grandfather, of course.

Grandfather's lunch of salmon in dill sauce with spring peas was eaten with great appreciation by Pinky and friends. I gave the mischief my portion too as I do not like salmon overmuch and the mischief is quite large. I didn't want anyone to feel left out or unappreciated. I think everyone got at least a nibble or two, but it was hard to tell and at one point my whole bedroom floor seemed to be covered with a living rug of rats.

I was too excited to be hungry, for now that Grandfather is gone, Mother will be coming home to live. I was so happy and content at the state of affairs I fell asleep to the warmth of Pinky's little ones snuggled up beneath my chin. Now I shall have to hide this account and do a better job than Josephine in The Crooked House, who was stupid enough to write *Today I killed Grandfather* in her diary which I couldn't write anyway because I did nothing of the sort, everything that happened is due to Grandfather's own bad heart.

***

Not long ago I woke to a terrible day with Pinky my only friend seemingly disappeared - and ended up with the most wonderful day ever, with five new friends. Today is just the opposite, I woke to a wonderful world in which Mother and I can now live together, but by the time the sun set it was a truly terrible day. There is a feeling of crackling paper and the edges of events aren't fitting together.

Mother is to be married! She told me herself when I brought her the breakfast tray. Maude is my witness,; she came along in the pocket of my jumper while Pinky nursed her pups. I can hardly believe it, Mother is to marry the Viscount Charles Mercy-Berginham of Culthroy. Mother said many times won't it be wonderful to be together again and she a peer of the realm. A peer is a member of the nobility in Britain, the home of my father.

I was quite upset by the news and retreated to my bed to read to Pinky and her darlings, an activity that always makes me feel calm. Tonight's story was The Adventure of the Clapham Cook written by Miss Agatha Christie, in which a man is killed and his body hidden in a great steamer trunk that is loaded onto a train, with porters lifting and carrying it and never suspecting a dead person was inside.

**

When I woke up this morning, Pinky's babies were nestled in my hair and ears while Pinky, Montague, Wimsey and a dozen others slept in the drawer and many more slept scattered on my coverlet and beneath it and all the rest on carpet. The sight gave me a happy, calm feeling but soon the peace was shattered by the arrival of three strangers - two women and a man whom Mother hired to clean the house.

I do not like interacting with strangers and stayed in the schoolroom working at my studies. Soon a cleaning man came all the way to the third floor - I clicked a warning to the mischief to hide just in time. He said his name was Avery and said good day to me, he was here to clean the fireplace. Now we can have a fire during lessons, I said and though I was talking to the mischief the man Avery said a nice fire was always welcoming to new home buyers.

His head was up in the chimney muffling his words so perhaps I did not hear him correctly, but before I could ask him to repeat himself he gave a great shout and there was a shower of sticks and leaves and bits of pages from old books and something fell from inside the chimney to land on the hearth.

In the fireplace was the most terrible sight I have ever seen. I tremble even to describe it. A great pile of dead rat pups with their tails all tangled up. I

186

counted nineteen pups, their fur was gray and dry and stiff.

Avery called it a rat king and showed me how the pups had become fused together. Together we gazed at it; when I went to lift it out of the fireplace Avery warned me not to touch it for fear of disease but leave it to the fumigators to take it away and burn it. Fumigation is the use of gaseous pesticides to poison pests.

After Avery left I lifted the rat king out of the fireplace so I could see it better; I clicked for the mischief to gather around. I had to be very careful to avoid snapping the dear desiccated little twig hands and feet. I could not stop looking at their little eyes closed as if sleeping. I could not understand why Avery called it nasty when it is so sad and beautiful, almost like a crown. Such a beautiful thing should never ever be burned.

This would have never happened, I told them, if Grandfather had not been so stingy, refusing to let us light a fire in the schoolroom. Look at what his stinginess has cost! I wept a bit and the mischief wept with me.

Everyone knows a king must have a queen, but Avery did not mention what a rat queen might be, nor is it an entry in the Encyclopedia Brittanica. I should like to say that I was very humble as I placed the crown on my head. The mischief crowded around, and separated to make a path for me as I made my way to my bedroom. I placed the rat king nestled in tissue paper in one of Mother's hat boxes for safekeeping under my bed and then slept like a queen, surrounded by her subjects.

***

More and more terrible news. Tonight at dinner I asked Mother what the man Avery could mean when he mentioned new home buyers. Mother became very cross and told me that a wife's place is with her husband, and a daughter's place was with her mother, which is why we are all moving to England to be with the Viscount, and where I am to go to boarding school.

Just writing these things has caused my condition to flare up. My eye twitch has returned. Mother stared at it while she told me she has already arranged with Mr. Archer to sell 7191 Stiles Street within a month's time. She said there is nothing to worry about as soon I will be the daughter of a Viscountess, a Viscountess being higher than a Baroness and people will have to call her My lady.

But Mother, I said, with Grandfather gone there is no impediment now, you can live here with me just like we have always wanted.

Mother said only that I am just like my Father, attached to this moldy old mansion never wanting to see the world. It is all very confusing and makes my head ache.

I have such a queer feeling, like bugs in my stomach. I've always believed Mother wants to live at 7191 Stiles Street. She said so herself - I never forget anything Mother tells me - that it would be wonderful to be just two women together against the world and not a husband in sight. But perhaps I was wrong like Sherlock Holmes in The Adventure of the Yellow Face.

***

On Thursday morning. in a state of high perturbation. I gathered my darlings in the schoolroom. The mischief has grown so that when they are all assembled for roll call they completely cover the school room floor, with even more flowing through the window from the roof. I explained Mother's plan to take me away from 7191 Stiles Street and there was much disconsolate squeaking. Disconsolate means without comfort.

Big Sam came from the roof, where the larger rats were gathered - some I have not yet made the acquaintance of - and bruxed a signal upon which those gathered on the floor separated themselves to form a little path to the door. To brux is to gnash one's teeth together. Down the hall I went, the way opening as I stepped along and into father's study, where the rat-cleared path led right to Father's old trunk in the corner.

Sam and Arther jumped on top of the trunk where Sam scratched for my attention; then Arthur ran down the side and disappeared. In a moment I heard his tiny scratching, this time from inside the trunk. I opened the trunk and there was Arthur! I clapped for my clever darling, but he was not just showing me a trick. Looking closely I could see a hole chewed through the trunk's side.

There was a canvas sack at the bottom of the trunk that contained almost nothing but holes plus a fluff of yellow hair and a gold chain with a thin round golden medallion with the initials GBM, just like the green leather covers on father's set of encyclopedias, just like the one in my only memory of father, the one Mother called a silly dream.

I knocked on Mother's door, though it was late. She tried to tell me she had a headache and we would talk tomorrow, but I felt I must be firm. I have something important to show you, I told her - a special gift from your husband!

I'm sorry to say that the mention of an odious husband engaged Mother's interest, causing her to unlock the door with alacrity. *Alacrity* is a brisk and cheerful readiness. The room was strewn about with clothing overflowing empty suitcases. Mother tried to close the door as soon as she saw what I wore but I am very slight and slipped through the door crack.

My God, said my mother who does not go to church. Take that *filthy* thing off your head, she said and upper her lip lifted when she said filthy like it knew what was about to happen and was trying to get away. I ignored the insult to my subjects as any queen wearing a crown would and should.

I lifted the medallion from where it hung around my neck.

See the initials GBM, Mother? For George Basil Mast, my father. I told you - a gift from your husband!

Together we watched the little circle of gold twist this way and that in the lamplight.

Where did you find that? Mother whispered. Her voice sounded like tiptoes on broken glass.

190

The same place I found this, I told her and held out the fluff of yellow hair. Mother became very pale. What do you want from me, she asked.

Although they were quiet, I could hear the mischief gathering behind the door and within the walls and peeping from under the bed. Mother did not notice; she looked from my queenly crown to my medallion, back and forth.

Impossible, she whispered.

I could think of no better quote than from Mr. Holmes's The Crooked Man, a favorite of Big Sam's.

When you have eliminated the impossible, whatever remains, however improbable, must be the truth, I declaimed, but it appears Mother and Big Sam do not share the same reading tastes for she seemed almost not to have heard me.

I said to Mother, The truth is, you killed father and locked his body in the trunk in his study, so that you could get his inheritance. You said you wanted nothing more than to stay in this house with me, but Grandfather prevented you.

But I need a dowry to marry the viscount, and this house is all we have, Mother said.

Very patiently I explained that it was mother herself who told me, a woman's place is with her husband, and a daughter's place was with her mother.

And that place is 7191 Stiles Street.

The mischief came out of hiding then, and Mother ran to the bathroom and locked herself in but of course the mischief had no trouble squeezing under the door, and swimming up from the toilet and the shower drain.

191

I became distressed at the sounds and so returned to my room, where Pinky nestled in my rolder while I read Miss Silver Deals with Death by Patricia Wenthworth. I read in a very loud voice but underneath the sound of the story could be heard the sound of the mischief as it moved something large and heavy sounding past my door that made wet thud thud sounds up the steps and into Father's study, where the great trunk stood open like a groom ready to receive its bride.

After many hours, the mischief returned to my room in little groups of twos and threes. They moved slowly as if tired, or full. Those with red droplets in their whiskers and staining their bellies were soon groomed by those that had stayed behind to keep me company.

When Mr. Archer calls - sent for via a courier - I will give him a letter from Mother. It is a very nice and detailed letter from My Lady Viscountess thanking Mr. Archer for ensuring that Miss Victoria's legacy continues to be paid out whilst she sets up house in Britain, a period of unknown duration. She explains how she plans to send for me once my studies are concluded with Professor Vreem, who is to be paid for this school term and the next at Mr. Archer's earliest convenience.

Mother asks in the letter that Mr. Archer leave certain paperwork - passwords and account numbers and such on the desk in Grandfather's study, the Viscount will send a courier to fetch it.

Mr. Archer will be full of congratulations for mother and me and full of plans for his very generous stipend he will receive when the paperwork is retrieved by the courier who is actually Big Sam and friends. A stipend is a fixed regular sum paid as a salary or allowance.

At some point I will send the mischief to blanket Mr. Archer in his bed. Big Sam will give his signal and they will gnaw through his wrists. The detectives will see the wounds and find the letter on his desk from one Viscountess Mercy-Berginham thanking him at the conclusion of many years of service. They will conclude Mr. Archer took his own life at the loss of his wealthiest client. Then it will just be me and Cook shopping and cooking and Housekeeper cleaning and Professor Vreems on Mondays, Tuesdays and Wednesdays. The rest of the week will be for as much mischief as we can make. According to the encyclopedia, that is quite a lot. Just two rats can produce 500,000 million pups in just three years. And to think the first thing they will see when they open their eyes is their Mischief Queen wearing her crown and welcoming them to our happy little kingdom at 7191 Stiles Street.

Very soon, one of these evenings I think I shall be strong enough to venture out, for even in my condition what possible bad can come to me surrounded by my friends? Perhaps we shall sail across the sea to Harrowden, me grand in a first class cabin with my stowaways safe in Father's trunk ready as I am to see what sort of mischief we can get up to.

Meet the Authors

Rie Sheridan Rose multitasks. A lot. Her short stories appear in numerous anthologies, including Killing It Softly Vol. 1 & 2, Hides the Dark Tower, Dark Divinations and On Fire. She has authored twelve novels, six poetry chapbooks and lyrics for dozens of songs. She is also editor-in-chief for Mocha Memoirs Press and editor for the Thirteen O' Clock imprint of Horrified Press. She tweets as @RieSheridanRose.

Liam A. Spinage is a former philosophy student, former archaeology educator and former police clerk who spends most of his spare time on the beach gazing up at the sky and across the sea while his imagination runs riot.

Sandra Stephens is a writer living in the Pacific Northwest with her husband and chocolate Labrador, Jake. She has published several shorts in the horror genre, and while she doesn't always write horror, she likes to imagine the most horrific turn of events in any circumstance, making her an excellent dinner party conversationalist.

SJ Townend hopes that her stories take the reader on a journey to often a dark place and only sometimes back again. SJ won the Secret Attic short story contest (Spring 2020), has had fiction published with Sledgehammer Lit Mag, Hash Journal, Ghost Orchid Press, Bandit Fiction, Black

Hare Press, Black Petals Horror Magazine, Ellipsis Zine, Gravely Unusual, Gravestone Press, Holy Flea, Horla Horror and was long listed for the Women on Writing non-fiction contest in 2020. She has also written and self-published two dark mystery novels, both of which are available to purchase elsewhere: (Tabitha Fox Never Knocks, Twenty-Seven and the Unkindness of Crows). Follow her on Twitter: @SJTownend

David Turnbull is a member of the Clockhouse London group of genre writers. He writes mainly short fiction and has had numerous short stories published in magazines and anthologies. His stories have previously been featured at Liars League London events and read at other live events such as Solstice Shorts and Virtual Futures. He was born in Scotland, but now lives in the Catford area of London. He can be found at www.tumsh.co.uk.

Lightning Source UK Ltd.
Milton Keynes UK
UKHW041110031222
413188UK00001B/74